The Niceness Quiz

"I can't believe it," Kate said, rolling on the floor with laughter. "Stephanie, you failed the niceness quiz! It's incredible! It's impossible!"

"I don't see what's so funny," I snapped. "You wouldn't be laughing if *you* had failed the quiz. How come you guys all came out nice, and I came out insensitive?"

"You probably just didn't understand the questions," Patti said reassuringly. "A lot of them were tricky."

"I've had enough!" I practically shouted. "I'm hungry and I'm going to the kitchen for more fudge."

"You're kidding. Ten minutes ago you said you were stuffed," Lauren reminded me.

"I changed my mind! A girl's allowed to change her mind, isn't she? Especially," I added sarcastically, "if she's as snobby and self-centered as me."

Look for these and other books in the Sleepover Friends Series:

The New Stephanie

Susan Saunders

AN
APPLE
PAPERBACK

SCHOLASTIC INC.
New York Toronto London Auckland Sydney

ISBN 0-590-43924-3

Copyright © 1991 by Daniel Weiss Associates, Inc. All rights reserved. Published by Scholastic Inc. APPLE PAPERBACKS is a registered trademark of Scholastic Inc. SLEEPOVER FRIENDS is a registered trademark of Daniel Weiss Associates, Inc.

12 11 10 9 8 7 6 5 4 3 2 1   1 2 3 4 5 6/9

Printed in the U.S.A.   28

First Scholastic printing, April 1991

Chapter
1

"You know, I'm really getting used to this health food stuff. One day I might even prefer it to our usual snacks," Lauren said as she read the ingredients label on her sugar-free, whole wheat cookies. "Want some, Stephanie?"

"No, thanks," I said, making a face. "I think they taste like dog biscuits. I don't see how you can eat them."

"They're good for you," Lauren protested. "And I have to eat *something*. I'm starving!"

Patti laughed. "You know Lauren. She's a human food disposal."

"I'll attest to that," Kate agreed. "If it's available, she'll eat it."

That was for sure. It didn't matter that I'd been watching Lauren Hunter eat like a horse for nearly

1

the past two years — her appetite at our sleepovers still amazed me.

Of course, the rest of us hadn't done so badly ourselves. I looked at the pile of wrappers, empty plates, and drained Dr Pepper float glasses scattered on my red-and-white tweed rug. As usual, we had pigged out at a sleepover.

Sleepovers, chocolate sundaes — you're probably wondering what's going on. Well, I'm Stephanie Green, and it's Friday night on Pine Street. That means Lauren Hunter, Patti Jenkins, Kate Beekman, and I are having one of our regular sleepovers. This one is at my house, and we're out in the backyard in my own private "apartment" — a playhouse that my parents built for me when my twin brother and sister were born.

See, the sleepovers started when Lauren and Kate were just little kids. They lived one house away from each other on Pine Street. That's practically next door. So, naturally, they became friends, back when the only thing that Lauren could eat came in a bottle.

The Sleepover Twins, as Kate's dad named them, spent their Friday nights playing games, dressing up, eating (of course), and watching movies on TV. They don't look anything like twins, though. Kate is short with blonde hair and blue eyes, and Lauren is tall with medium brown hair and hazel eyes.

The twosome became a threesome when I

2

moved to Pine Street from the city the summer before fourth grade. Lauren and I met in Mr. Civello's class, 4A, and we hit it off right away. It was another story with Kate, though. When Lauren invited me to one of their sleepovers, Kate and I clashed about almost everything! Maybe because we're too much alike. Both of us know what we want and don't mind telling everyone. I wouldn't call us bossy . . . well, maybe a *little*. I prefer to describe us as "in control" or "together."

But Lauren is pretty persistent (*stubborn* actually), and she kept throwing us together until we began to see past that first meeting. Now I'm so glad that Kate Beekman is my friend. She's come through for me plenty of times.

And then there's Patti Jenkins. She was the last to join the group. Patti and I are so different that it's kind of funny we went to the same school in the city when we were in first grade. I'm outgoing. Patti's shy. I love fashion and am a real shopaholic. Patti would rather read a book than worry about clothes. And I'm short, like Kate, and Patti's even taller than Lauren. She has brown hair and brown eyes.

When we're all together, Patti is the calm over any possible storms that Kate or I might start. If Lauren can't make us see reason, Patti usually can.

Together we make a fantastic foursome. We sure have done some fun things, like spy on slippery magicians, and rescue Lauren's dog, Bullwinkle, when he raced across town to the Pine Street house that they used to live in before they moved.

Oops, that's another thing. A little while ago, Lauren moved across town, almost two miles away, to Brio Drive. At first she hated it. We all did. But it turned out to be better than we thought.

We all still go to the same school, and we all still ride our bikes there together. And Lauren has this new, really cool bed that she paid for by working at Alice's Attic, this adorable secondhand furniture store. (I worked there, too, and bought a black, white, and red rocking zebra for Emma and Jeremy.)

But enough of that. Back to the sleepover.

That night we had talked about playing Mad Libs or Truth or Dare, or possibly this new board game that Patti found called GirlGab.

"What time is it?" I wondered suddenly. I jumped up to look at the digital clock on the VCR. "Oh, no, I wanted to watch *A Time for Love*." Kevin DeSpain is in it and he's my all-time favorite actor.

"Do we have to?" Kate asked. "I'd rather watch *Tales of a Teenage Werewolf* on Channel 24. It's an old black-and-white horror movie — a real classic."

"Yuck." Lauren made a face. "Sometimes those classics that you're so hooked on turn out to be class-A duds."

"Shows how much you know," Kate retorted. "This is the very first movie where they actually show the man changing into the wolf. It was very high tech for its time."

"If you say so," Lauren said. Lauren hates were-wolf movies almost as much as she hates vampire movies. She flipped open my latest copy of *Teen Topics* magazine.

"Besides, you've seen that movie a million times," I reminded Kate. "I'd rather watch Kevin DeSpain." I turned on the set and waited as it warmed up before I changed the channel.

"Hey," Lauren said, turning to the center section of the magazine. "Here's a great new quiz."

"What kind?" Kate asked, leaning over for a closer look.

"It's called, 'Are You Nice? Or Not?' " Lauren said. "It's about friendship — so it's perfect for us, the best friends in the whole world. Right?"

"Let's take it," Patti said, smiling.

"What about the movie?" I wailed. "The credits are already starting to roll."

"Tape it," Patti said. "Then we can watch it later when we run out of quizzes and games."

She had a point, I thought, as I popped a blank tape into the VCR and pushed the record button. I turned off the picture just as Kevin DeSpain's gor-

5

geous, smiling face appeared on the screen.

"Okay, I'm ready," I said, plopping down on the rug.

Lauren handed us each a piece of paper and a pencil. Then she read, " 'Friendships are wonderful, but it takes a lot of energy to keep them running smoothly. How nice you are has everything to do with how many friends you have and the way people see you. How nice are you? Score your niceness quotient, then learn how you can be a better buddy and a better person all around.' "

"Sounds boring," I said, still thinking about having to turn off my movie.

"C'mon," Lauren said. "This will be easy for us. Just think if it were Ginger Kinkaid taking the quiz. I mean, we all know what kind of score she would get on the Friend-o-Meter."

We all laughed. "Not very high," Kate said. "Unless there was something in it for her."

Ginger Kinkaid had tried to break up our group when she first moved to town, by latching onto Lauren and trying to be her only best friend. Then she met Christy Soames, who's a real fashion plate, and Ginger dropped Lauren like a hot potato. We avoid Ginger whenever we can, which is pretty difficult since her parents got a divorce and she moved with her mom into Lauren's old house on Pine Street!

"First question," Kate said, grabbing the book from Lauren and getting back to the point. " 'Your friend flunked a math test and she's really upset about it. What do you do? A: Tell her she never would have gotten herself into this mess if she'd spent more time studying. If she's failing, it's her own fault.' "

Everybody groaned. I thought that was a good answer. But I wouldn't decide until I'd heard all of the other choices.

Kate continued. " 'B: Jokingly tell her that the batteries must be dead on her calculator. That, or her brain. You change the subject to help her get her mind off of her troubles.' "

This time we all laughed as we waited for Kate to read the third choice.

" 'C: You offer to help her with her homework or find a tutor who can.' "

Boring, boring, boring, I thought. Gosh, if I tutored everybody who was having trouble in math, I'd never get my own studying done. I guess I'm lucky that Kate, Lauren, and especially Patti, get pretty good grades in school.

I marked down "A" because "B" was too rude and "C" was too obvious.

Patti read the next question. " 'If someone gossiped to you about another friend, would you: A: Immediately relate the information to your friend?

B: Pass on the tidbit to the rest of the school? Or C: Tell the blabbermouth that you don't listen to rumors?' "

Well, that was a tough one. Normally I tell gossipers to keep their rumors to themselves. Gossip can get you into trouble. But, on the other hand, if someone started a rumor about one of my Sleepover pals, I'd probably tell them right away so that we could do something to have the rumor stopped. Sleepover Friends stick together.

I marked "A" again. I wondered what answers the others were marking. But when I craned my neck I couldn't read their papers.

We passed the magazine around, asking the rest of the questions: *What do you do if your friend runs for class president and loses?* and *What do you say on a shopping trip if your friend asks your opinion on a dress that makes her look like an elephant?*

Then there were: *Are you a generally positive person? When asked to make a comment, can you usually find something nice to say?* And, my personal favorite: *How often do you let others borrow your clothes or your money?*

The quiz asked how we felt when we woke up in the morning. I answered that I was ready to smash the alarm clock when it went off. I wasn't sure how to answer the question about what I would do if someone tried to push me into something I didn't want to do. I mean, it would depend on who they were and their relationship to me, right? And what they were asking me to do. I mean, for sure I wouldn't go for a ride with a stranger. But, I had turned off the TV that night, hadn't I?

As far as I was concerned, the questions weren't as easy to answer as A, B, or C.

The magazine came around to me again and I looked to see how many more questions there were. Three. Thank goodness this was almost over. I pushed my dark, curly bangs out of my face and read the question out loud:

" 'When I'm with my friends: A: I find myself wondering if I'd rather be in the popular crowd. B: I always have the best time! There's no place I'd rather be. Or C: I always wonder if they like me as much as I like them.' "

I might as well be completely honest. I had been up until then with my answers. I marked "C." Oh, sure, I have a great time with my friends, but sometimes I wonder. . . .

The last question was, *How much time do you spend each week improving your community and/or doing things for others?*

Not much, I thought as I checked off my final answer. After all, we had school, homework, and so on.

Lauren read off the score key and I tallied up

my answers. The best score was 19–22 points. Of course Patti received 22 out of 22 points. No surprise there. Patti is the nicest person we know.

" 'Hurray,' " Lauren read. " 'Lucky you! You must be on top of the world! You can't help it. Niceness is your habit. Better yet, your sunshine personality means you're always surrounded by a group of friends who are also full of cheer. Congratulations!' "

"Wow, Patti. I didn't come close to perfection," Lauren said. "I only got eighteen points." For that score, the magazine said, " 'You are optimistic and ready for opportunities to practice your niceness on anyone you meet. You're sure to lead a long and happy, fulfilling life.' "

Kate got 15 points. No problem. The score key said, " 'You're as near nice as you can be. You haven't reached the ultimate degree, but you're well on your way. All you have to do is make more time for things and people that are important to you.' "

"So what did you get?" Kate asked me. "I hope your score is keeping mine company. I don't want to be a niceness washout all by myself." Kate laughed and socked me in the arm. "Hey, we all knew no one could be as nice as Patti."

"That's for sure." I laughed, too, hoping that no one would notice how bugged I was by my score. "I got a nine."

"A nine!" Lauren shrieked. "I can't believe it. Poor Stephenie!"

Kate grinned. "What did you do, mark the wrong scores on purpose?"

"I was just being honest," I said, hands on my hips.

"Sure you were," Patti joked, joining the others in teasing me.

"Here, let me read Stephanie's niceness quotient. *'What's putting a hold on your niceness?'* " Lauren read. " *'You must have a lot of empty spaces on your calendar. Someone as self-centered, insensitive, and snobby as you couldn't possibly have any fun. Who would want to be friends with you, anyway?'* "

"I can't believe it," Kate said, rolling on the floor with laughter. "Stephanie failed the niceness quiz! It's incredible! It's impossible!"

"I don't see what's so funny," I snapped. "You wouldn't be laughing if you failed the quiz."

Lauren put her arm around my shoulder, but she was laughing so hard that she couldn't keep a straight face. "It's all a joke," she told me. "These quizzes don't mean anything. The answers are rigged."

"Then how come you guys all came out nice, and I came out insensitive?" I wanted to know.

"You probably just didn't understand the questions," Patti said reassuringly. "A lot of them were tricky."

Trust Patti to see the positive side. Still, she was laughing almost as hard as the rest of them.

"Fine! I've had enough!" I practically shouted. "I'm hungry and I'm going to the kitchen for more fudge."

"You're kidding. Ten minutes ago you said you were stuffed," Lauren reminded me.

"I changed my mind! A girl's allowed to change her mind, isn't she? Especially," I added sarcastically, "if she's as snobby and self-centered as me."

My last comment sent them into renewed fits, and the sound of their laughter followed me all the way across the lawn and into the house.

Chapter 2

Maybe Lauren, Kate, and Patti thought the niceness quiz was all a big joke, but I worried about it. Up until then I had thought of myself as cheerful, outgoing, and a little opinionated. But maybe I was really snobby, insensitive, and self-centered!

I joined in the games and chatter for the rest of the evening, but my mind was on the results of that quiz. I lay awake long after our final game of Mad Libs and after we watched *A Time for Love*. Not even Kevin DeSpain cheered me up.

Listening to the breathing of my three best friends sleeping near me, I began to wonder: Did they really like me as much as I liked them? Did they really think the niceness quiz was just a joke? Or — had I been set up? Maybe they'd suggested the quiz because they thought I needed a few hints about my personality!

The moon rose outside my playhouse window.

13

I stared at it as I thought back on all the times I could have been nicer. Like when Lauren found out she had to move. I probably could have been more sympathetic. And when the twins were born, I really gave my parents a hard time. Even lately, I hadn't been helping out as much as I probably should.

I had to face it: I tend to think of me first, and then the rest of the world.

Starting the next day, I decided that was going to change. I was going to become the nicest, most generous, most unselfish fifth-grader in town. According to the *Teen Topics* quiz, I had to do something quick, or else I would end up losing my friends.

That would be awful. Lauren, Kate, and Patti were so special. I couldn't bear to think that I wasn't worthy of them. How had they put up with my terrible attitude for almost two years? It just showed how wonderfully nice they all were. They had been too nice to tell me about my flaws.

Even now, they didn't come right out and say I was on the verge of losing their friendship. Instead, they had made sure we all took the niceness quiz so that I would see for myself.

I finally fell asleep around dawn, still thinking of ways I could improve my niceness quotient and become a better friend.

The next day Lauren suggested a trip to the mall,

normally my favorite hangout on Saturdays, but I made up an excuse not to go.

"Are you feeling all right, Stephanie?" Kate asked. "It's not like you to turn down shopping."

"I have to go to the library," I said vaguely. "I'm doing some research."

After they left, I asked Mom if I could ride my bike to the library.

"Sure," she said, juggling Emma on one knee and Jeremy on the other. "Just be back before two o'clock. I'd like to get this place cleaned up before our dinner guests arrive tonight."

"You can count on me," I said. "Don't worry, I'll help you get this place in shape."

It was kind of interesting to see Mom's reaction to my offer of help. She looked closely at me to make sure I wasn't ill.

I smiled inside. I *could* be nice if I wanted to.

At the library I checked out all the books on improving your personality. My stack of titles included, *How to Make Friends*; *Being a Good Friend*; *Positive Thinking the Easy Way*; *It's Nice to Be Nice*; and *Highway to Happiness*.

Wow, I thought. I must not be the only one who needs help becoming a nicer person. I flipped open *It's Nice to Be Nice* and read the list of rules on the first page.

Do: Spend quality time with your friends.

Do: Speak only if you have something nice to say.

Do: Give service — to your community, your friends, your parents, and to all those in need. Find a way to help.

Do: Say "yes" more than "no."

Do: Think of others first. Making others happy is nice.

Do: Follow through on your commitments.

Do: Smile — a lot.

This was going to be easy. I remembered the smile on Mom's face when I offered to help her clean the house later. *Give a little, get a lot.* That was going to be my niceness motto from now on. The Sleepover Friends wouldn't have any reason not to want me for a friend.

I smiled at the librarian as she checked out my books. "I'd like to do some community service," I told her cheerfully. "Do you have any suggestions, or know where I could find a list of volunteer opportunities?"

"As a matter of fact, I have just the thing for you," she said. She pointed to a poster.

" 'Save the Library,' " I read aloud. "What's that all about?"

"The library needs volunteers to collect contributions and used books for the annual library drive," the librarian told me. "All you have to do is talk to your neighbors and friends and give out our fundraising leaflets."

"That's perfect," I said. "I'll do it." I took a stack of leaflets and added them to the books in my backpack. My campaign for niceness was off to a good start.

For the rest of the weekend I practiced being nice. I helped my parents without being asked. I did all of my homework, and even played with Emma and Jeremy so that Mom and Dad could enjoy visiting with their dinner guests.

On Sunday, loaded with leaflets, I set out to do my volunteer job for the library.

It was kind of scary. I'm certainly not shy, but I had never asked anyone for donations before. *What if they think I'm just going to steal their money?* I thought worriedly as I walked up to the first house.

I reached for the doorbell and hesitated. I wished that my friends were with me. But I had picked a different street on purpose so that I couldn't accidentally run into them. I wanted my niceness plan to be a secret.

Okay, I'm going to do it, I told myself. I reached out and rang the bell.

"Hi," I said to the lady who opened the door.

I gave her a big smile. "I'm Stephanie Green and I'm collecting old books and contributions for the Save the Library drive. Would you like to contribute?"

My knees felt like jelly as she read the leaflet that I handed to her. I forced myself to take two deep breaths.

"I'm sure I can find a few books to donate," she said, smiling back at me. "You wait there, Stephanie, and I'll be right back."

I sagged back against her wall. I had done it! My first house! After that it became easier. Most of the people were happy to help. I passed out all of the leaflets and collected twenty-two dollars in pledges for the library fund.

By the time I met up with the gang on Monday morning at the corner of Hillcrest and Pine, I was feeling pretty good about the new, nicer me.

As usual, I had gotten up early enough to make sure I looked good, too. I was wearing my best black jeans and a new red top that had feathery white fringe down the sleeves. I had pulled my hair back in a neat ponytail and had wrapped it with red and white ribbons.

But I knew a nice person doesn't care if anyone notices what *she* is wearing. Instead, she makes other people feel good about themselves.

"You look great in that yellow sweater," I complimented Patti. She was the first one there. "It brings out the highlights in your hair."

"Really?" Patti said with a smile. "I thought it made my face look yellow."

"Not at all," I assured her. "You look as rosy-cheeked and healthy as ever."

"Well . . . thanks." She put her hands up to her cheeks. "I think."

Kate and Lauren rode up at almost the same time, Kate's short, blonde hair and Lauren's brown hair blowing in the wind.

"Great outfit, Lauren," I said. "Love the red overalls."

"Thanks. I bought them at Just Juniors when we went to the mall on Saturday. There was a pair in your size, and a neat black-and-white T-shirt to go with it."

"I'll have to check it out," I said. "Thanks for thinking of me."

It was great to have friends who knew your style. Mine has been red, black, and white for quite a while now. My clothes, my room, even my binders and notepads, are in those great colors. Some people might think wearing combinations of only three colors is limiting or boring, but not me. I think it makes my wardrobe much more interchangeable.

Take my fringed red top, for example. I had

19

about ten different outfits I could wear it with. It gave me a lift just thinking about it.

I looked at Kate, hunched over her handlebars, weighed down by her heavy backpack. She had been sick for a couple of days last week and I knew she had had to make up the homework over the weekend.

"Can I help you carry some of that junk?" I asked. "I don't have many books this morning." I didn't mention the five pounds of library leaflets.

Kate perked up right away, then looked at me a little suspiciously. "Are you serious?"

"Of course!" I exclaimed. "Give me half, then the ride to school will be much more enjoyable for all of us."

I breathed deeply as we started pedaling down Hillcrest. I was in the lead, then came Patti, then Lauren and Kate. The cool morning air was refreshing. Just like it said in the *Teen Topics* quiz, I was looking forward to a bright new life.

"What a glorious day!" I called back to the others. "I'm so lucky to have such good friends and be going to such a good school! This week is going to be great — I can tell."

"Stephanie, are you feeling okay?" Patti asked. "You're not acting like your . . . uh . . . usual self this morning."

By "usual" I knew she meant grumpy, bossy,

snobby, self-centered, and insensitive. I had a long way to go before I became as nice as Patti. The books and practice would help. Volunteering for the library gave me a good feeling. So did complimenting my friends.

But I didn't want to tell them about my niceness plan. Instead, I said sincerely, "I'm feeling absolutely wonderful, Patti. Thanks for asking."

Being nice isn't always so easy, I found out later that morning. In Mrs. Mead's class, 5B, I sit in the very first row, Kate and Lauren sit in back of me, and poor Patti is stuck way back in the last desk of the last row.

Mrs. Mead was passing out the results of the annual achievement tests and Kate started cracking jokes. "I'm glad I'm not Wayne Miller's mother," she whispered. "It would be so depressing to realize your son is a Neanderthal!"

Lauren snickered. "Look on the bright side. He brings the grading curve down for the whole state!"

Wayne Miller *is* a dud in the true sense of the word. Not to mention his gross habits, like burping in class. None of us are even sure how he made it as far as fifth grade, except that his teachers probably passed him on because they didn't want to see his face for another year.

"Wayne's so dumb he probably needs help

going to the — " I started to say, then I stopped myself just in time. Insulting people wasn't nice. Neither was gossiping. What about that rule about saying something nice or nothing at all?

"What did you say?" Lauren whispered.

"Uh, nothing," I lied. "I was just saying that I'm sure Wayne has some really good qualities. You just have to look harder for them than with most people."

Kate's mouth dropped open. She and Lauren stared at each other in amazement.

"Are you sure you're all right?" Kate asked. "Did you fall and hit your head over the weekend?"

"I'm fine. I just think we should give Wayne a chance, that's all."

Saying something nice about Wayne Miller was one of the hardest things I've ever done. My smile probably looked more like a grimace, but at least I tried.

I looked at the scores on my computer printout. Average, just as I expected. I was working at, or slightly above, fifth-grade level in each of my subjects. Not a genius, but not a flop, either. I wondered what scores some of the other kids in the class received.

I didn't have long to wait.

Jenny Carlin announced hers to the class. "Look at this," she said, her voice carrying to our side of the classroom. "I've been looking forward to finding out my results. I scored between sixth and eighth grade in everything. Do you know what that means?" she asked her best buddy, Angela Kemp. "It means I'll be skipped into sixth grade."

"You don't know that," Kate told her. Privately I knew Kate was hoping Jenny *would* be moved a grade ahead. Jenny's as obnoxious as Wayne is stupid.

Jenny pretended she didn't hear Kate's comment. "Anyone can see that I belong with a more advanced group," she said snobbily.

"That's true, Jenny," Angela agreed. "I've always known that. You're more advanced than anyone I know."

Yeah, I wish she'd advance out into the hall, I thought. But I kept my mouth shut. This nice stuff was turning out to be harder than I'd thought!

The final bell rang, and Mrs. Mead put up her hand for quiet before we all began loading our backpacks to go home.

"Would Jennifer Carlin, Patricia Jenkins, Tina Martin, and Michael Pastore please see me for a few minutes after school? The rest of you are dismissed."

Lauren had a worried frown on her face. "I wonder what that's all about? You don't think Patti's in trouble, do you?"

23

"Are you kidding?" Kate said. "Patti never gets into trouble."

"I'm sure she's just going to compliment Patti and the others on their high marks," I said. "C'mon, we'll wait in the hall for Patti to come out."

Chapter
3

Patti looked very worried when she came out of the classroom a few minutes later.

"What's wrong, Patti? Your test scores were okay, weren't they?" I asked.

Patti held the printout of her scores in her hand as if it were a strange object from another world. With it was a yellow conference request notice.

"I don't understand," she said. "Mrs. Mead told us that we all did really well on the achievement tests. But she wants our parents to come in for conferences. I thought they only did that when you needed improvement."

The rest of us were as puzzled as Patti.

Kate tried to crack the somber mood with a joke. "Maybe you're a behavior problem," she teased.

"Or maybe Mrs. Mead just wants your parents to hear the good report in person," I said, shaking my head at Kate. *Sometimes Kate doesn't know when to quit,* I thought as I laid my hand on Patti's shoulder. Anyone with sensitivity could see that Patti needed sympathy right then, not jokes. "Do you want us to go with you to tell your parents? Sleepover Friends stick together. We won't let you go through this alone."

"Thanks, Stephanie," Patti said.

"Yeah, and on the way we can stop at Charlie's Soda Fountain and buy a frozen juice bar," Lauren suggested. "Refreshing and healthy." Lauren, the snack queen of Riverhurst, was still on her health-food kick.

"That sounds good," Patti agreed with a small smile.

As we unlocked our bikes and rode off, I could tell that Patti was still worried. She had that little frown on her face that she gets when she's thinking hard about something.

I tried to think of a way to make her feel better. I was determined that the new kinder and more sensitive Stephanie would do everything she could to help her friend.

As it turned out, the Jenkinses weren't home when we arrived — after having stopped at Charlie's for a quick treat. Patti told us there was nothing we could do by hanging out at her house, so we reluctantly rode to our own homes.

* * *

There also wasn't much to speculate about on the way to school the next day because Patti's conference wasn't scheduled until later that afternoon. We would just have to wait and see.

Between school and the notes we passed, we managed to keep Patti's mind off her worries until lunch. Then Jenny Carlin had to open her big mouth. "I can't wait until my parent-teacher conference this afternoon," she said loudly to Angela as she passed our table in the cafeteria. "I can't wait until I get passed into sixth grade."

"Neither can we," Kate remarked just loud enough for Jenny and Angela to hear.

Jenny spun around and flashed us a stuck-up grin. "You fifth-graders are so immature. I'm glad I'm leaving you behind."

"Not as glad as the rest of us *immature* fifth-graders," Kate said sarcastically.

I started to giggle, but clapped my hand over my mouth just in time.

"You're just jealous!" Jenny shot back.

"Am not!" Kate said.

"Are too!"

"Quiet, Kate," I whispered. "You two shouldn't argue about something that hasn't happened yet. I'm sure Jenny will fill us in on all of the details as soon as she finds out. And I'm sure Mrs. Mead and her

27

parents will do what's best for Jenny's education."

Kate frowned at me. "Why are you stopping me?" she asked. "I was just getting started."

"It's not worth fighting about, that's all," I told her.

Jenny flipped her hair over her shoulder and stuck her nose about as far up in the air as she could raise it. Angela copied her, but she didn't look nearly as happy as Jenny.

"At least there's one sensible person at your table," Jenny pronounced. "So long, you guys. I hope you have fun staying in 5B, *as in baby*, fifth grade."

Jenny's attitude really made me mad. I felt like telling her what I thought of her. But I was saved from breaking my vow of niceness because just then Hope Lenski joined us.

Hope moved to Riverhurst just before Valentine's Day, so we haven't known her that long. She was quiet at first, and she wears strange clothes and eats only health food, so everyone thought she was weird. But she's turned out to be a special friend — she's even come to some of our sleepovers. *And,* she's also the one kid I know who spends time trying to improve the community and the environment. Maybe she would have some ideas for me.

"What's up, Hope?" I asked. She opened her lunch box and took out a banana, a peanut butter-

and-apple butter sandwich on whole wheat bread, and a thermos of milk.

"I just came over to see how you guys are doing. I've been so busy working for the recycling center that I haven't had a chance to catch up on the latest news."

"Well, I for one am doing just great," I said. "And this is the best cafeteria lunch ever. Mmm." I bit into my deep-fried burrito as Hope wrinkled her nose.

Kate leaned over to feel my forehead. "What's gotten into you, Steph?"

"Nothing. I'm just saying that the food is good today. No meat, just beans," I added for Hope's benefit. Hope is a vegetarian.

"Oh, that's good," Hope said, smiling. She took a big bite of her sandwich.

"Tell us about the recycling center," Lauren said. "What do you do there?"

"Well, people bring in their cans, bottles, and newspapers. We smash the cans, weigh them, and write up a ticket so that the people can get their money. I answer phones and give people prices per pound for their glass and newspapers and stuff."

"Sounds interesting," I said. "I've been doing a neat community project, too." I smiled inwardly, knowing they were going to be surprised.

"Is that what you were doing all weekend?" Patti asked. "You haven't said much about it."

"Well, I went around on Sunday asking for donations of old books for the Library Book Sale, and for contribution pledges for the Save the Library drive."

"Why didn't you tell us?" Lauren said. "Is that why you couldn't go to the mall with us?"

"Well . . . sort of," I hedged. I didn't want to tell them the real reason I went to the library in the first place. "Yeah, I went to the library that day. So, will you guys go through your old books and let me know if you have any to donate to the library? They need everyone's help."

"Sure, no problem," Patti said. "I have a lot of books that could be *recycled,* so to speak."

"Me, too," Lauren chimed in.

"Are you going to be doing this every weekend, or will you be able to go shopping with us sometime?" Kate wanted to know.

Before I could say anything, Jenny Carlin, at the table in back of us, started laughing. "Gee, it's too bad the achievement test wasn't in shopping, Stephanie," she joked loudly. "You would have come out first!"

I turned around, ready to bash her. What was her problem, anyway? We weren't bothering her. We weren't even talking to her.

30

I was about to say, *Do you practice being rude, or does it just come naturally?* I bit my lip instead.

"Are you going to just sit there and take that?" Kate asked incredulously.

I didn't say anything. I took a deep breath and tried to concentrate on my burrito. It's really hard to be nice sometimes. I mean *really, really* hard.

Kate turned to Jenny and spoke for me. "Don't you know it's rude to eavesdrop on other people's conversations?"

"Who's eavesdropping? You guys are loud enough that the whole cafeteria can hear you!"

Oooh! Was I ready to tell Jenny Carlin a thing or two! But I had promised myself I was going to change. Even if Jenny *did* have the loudest mouth this side of the Rocky Mountains.

I had to stop Kate before she and Jenny got into a full-scale argument. "Never mind," I told Kate through clenched teeth. "What Jenny said isn't worth fighting over. She's allowed to have her own opinion."

"I can't believe you!" Kate said, hitting her forehead with the heel of her hand. "First you defend Wayne, and now Jenny."

Jenny was listening very carefully to what Kate was saying. I wanted to tell her to turn around and mind her own business, but I forced myself to smile at her instead.

"It's no big deal," I said to both Kate and Jenny. I made myself do a short laugh. "It's no secret that I like to shop."

Jenny's eyes narrowed suspiciously. I could tell she wasn't used to people other than Angela agreeing with her. It made me feel kind of powerful inside. Niceness was a great thing. You could change enemies into friends — well, maybe not *friends* exactly, but not such bad enemies — with just a smile or a kind word. Just think what I could do for the community!

Of course my friends thought I had gone a little crazy. Several times I caught them looking at me thoughtfully, trying to figure out what was going on.

They would get used to the new me, though. I was sure they would like the new me better. After all, they had suggested we do the quiz, giving me the hint to change in the first place.

Later on that day, my niceness campaign paid off again. We were all standing on the front steps of the school, waiting for Patti's parents to arrive, when Hope burst through the double doors.

"I've been looking for you," she told us. "Would you guys like to come with me to the recycling center today? I just talked to them on the phone and they said the Boy Scouts brought in a huge load of aluminum cans today. They could use some extra help."

32

"I'm sorry," Patti said. "I have to stay after school for my parent-teacher conference."

"How about you, Stephanie?" Hope asked. "I especially thought you might want to, since you seem to enjoy helping the community."

My plan was working! Already Hope thought I was a kind, helpful person.

I grinned. "Sure, I'd love to come. I have to call my mom, but I know she won't mind. What about you two?" I asked, turning to Lauren and Kate. "It would be a great opportunity to do some community service!"

Kate yawned, and Lauren shuffled around the books and papers in her backpack. "What do you think, Lauren?" Kate asked. "We don't have that much homework tonight, so we could probably do it for a little while."

"I guess," Lauren said, zipping the final pocket on her backpack and hoisting it onto her shoulders. "I don't have anything else better to do."

"C'mon," I said, hopping on my bike and ignoring their less-than-enthusiastic responses. "It'll be fun!"

Chapter
4

We made a quick stop at the pay phone to call our parents for permission, and then we rode the short distance to the Riverhurst Recycling Center. It was a large mobile home set up in the parking lot of Compton's Grocery Store. When we arrived, there was already a lot of activity going on.

"These are my friends, Stephanie, Kate, and Lauren," Hope told the girl who was checking in the volunteers. "What do you want us to do?"

"I'm pleased to meet you," she said. "My name is Barbara, and I'm the coordinator here. We're always glad to see more volunteers."

Before we did anything, Barbara gave us a tour. There were huge colorful posters describing everything from the disposal of toxic waste to the hole in the ozone layer caused by fluorocarbons in things like hairspray and spray-paint cans.

I felt glad that I used styling gel in a tube. And that my family sometimes turns in our aluminum cans. I decided I would have to give recycling more thought when I went home.

I was very impressed with the displays, and with Barbara. She knew so much about saving the environment, especially about little things that add up to big wastes if everyone does them. "What do you think?" she asked with a smile.

"I can't wait to get started," I said, returning her smile. "What do we do first?"

"I'm sure Hope has told you that we don't allow our younger volunteers to work any of the machines, but we need some help loading the crushed cans into the storage bins. And if you finish with that, our monthly newsletter needs to be folded, stapled, and labeled for mailing."

"Let's get to work," I said, heading toward the pile of crushed cans she pointed at. "Grab a shovel, you three. We have a lot of aluminum to load."

I marched out in front of the group, carrying my shovel on my shoulder and feeling great about having the opportunity to help. Why hadn't I been doing this sort of thing all along? I really *had* been selfish and self-centered. There was a whole world out there that I had been missing.

Everyone at the RRC was really nice. All of the older, high-school-age volunteers had a smile or a joke for us when they brought us more cans. They made us feel like part of the group. I think even Kate and Lauren began to like it after awhile.

Shoveling cans into the storage bins — which are called hoppers — was hard work. It was dirty work, too. Almost immediately, my new white pants and red shirt were covered with sticky dirt from the cans. I really hate getting my clothes dirty, but I told myself it was for a good cause.

Sweat poured down my face as I scooped cans and lifted them into the bins. Every time I thought we were done, someone brought over another load and dumped it at our feet. There was no way we were going to get to the newsletter.

But I tried to keep smiling. With every shovelful, I told myself that a person had to occasionally do things she didn't want to do in order to be nice. *Someone* had to do this job. If my clothes got a little dirty, so what? Next time I would wear my old grubby jeans and a shirt I didn't care about. And pull my hair back into a bandanna.

I reached up gingerly to touch my hair. Yuk. It was sticking out all over. I hoped it wouldn't be permanently frizzed. I was glad only Kate, Lauren, and Hope were there to see me looking so awful.

"You girls have done a fantastic job today," Barbara said after we had been going at it for about an hour. "Why don't we call it a day?"

We all leaned on our shovels and wiped the sweat off our foreheads.

"I'm sorry we didn't have time to help you with your newsletter," I told her.

"That's okay," Barbara said. "We'll get it done eventually. It will probably be late going out, as usual."

"Not necessarily," I said, coming up with another great idea. "I could come back some other day and just work on the newsletter. Would that help?"

"That would help a lot," Barbara told me. "Why don't we sign you up to come on the same days as Hope? You could ride over together."

"Great idea," I said. "Where do I sign?"

I followed Barbara over to her coordinator's table and filled out a card with my name and address on it. What a perfect opportunity to be unselfish and giving! I was well on the way to making my plan work. I had to admit I liked the way people responded to the new, nicer me. I felt more important, somehow.

"That was really nice of you to volunteer, Steph," Kate said when I rejoined them.

Even Kate is noticing, I thought happily. I had to stop myself before I said something that sounded like bragging, though. I just said, "Oh, thanks. I think it will be very rewarding."

Before long, I wouldn't have to worry anymore

37

about losing my Sleepover Friends. I would be as nice as them. All I had to do was stick to the plan.

My plan included helping out and being more agreeable at home, too. After dinner, Mom started taking things out of the kitchen cupboards and wiping off the shelves.

"What are you doing, Mom?" I asked. "Did something spill?"

"No. I'm just tired of the clutter. I open up a door and I can't find anything. See," she said triumphantly, "here's the set of salt shakers that I've been trying to find for months. They were right here all along, hidden behind these old boxes of cereal."

I peered into the other cupboards. Each one was as cluttered as the one Mom was working on. Of course, how could it be any different? Mom had the whole house to take care of, not to mention the twins, me, and Dad. She didn't have time for organizing cupboards.

I had been really selfish, I thought guiltily. All I did was come home, eat dinner, and if I cleaned anything, it was my *own* room. I used my homework as an excuse not to help with the housework.

"Need some help?" I volunteered. "I could stand on the counter and hand you stuff."

"That would be wonderful, Stephanie," Mom said. "This kind of a job is much more fun with company."

It *was* fun — sort of. Well, it was fun hanging out with Mom. Dad kept Jeremy and Emma entertained in the living room, so it was the first time in a long time that we had a chance to talk without one or more babies around.

It didn't make me love housework, though. I hated cleaning and scrubbing. I always have and probably always will. A little while ago, the Sleepover Friends had needed to make money for an extra ticket to Wilderness World, and I certainly did my share of window-washing and yard work. But I had hated it. Still, I could tell that my helping had made Mom happy. That was the important part.

"How was your afternoon at the recycling center?" Mom wanted to know.

I handed her two almost-empty jars of honey. "It was . . . educational," I explained. "We helped load crushed aluminum cans into storage hoppers. People sure drink a lot of soda."

"It's a good thing that aluminum is recyclable," Mom remarked as she wiped off the flour canister and handed it back up to me.

"Yeah, but you wouldn't believe how much aluminum there is that *doesn't* get recycled," I began excitedly. "Over eighty percent ends up on roadsides or in landfills. Do you know that if twenty-two million people — not even ten percent of America — recycled one soda can each day for a week, there'd be more than three thousand tons of aluminum recycled? And that means a lot less aluminum ending up in dumps." I quoted one of the posters that I had read at the recycling center.

"And those plastic six-pack rings. They're the worst. We should always remember to cut them in half before we dispose of them. Animals in the wild get their heads stuck in them and then they die from strangulation." I felt so knowledgeable — so grown up.

"That's awful," Mom said. "I didn't know that."

"That's not even half of it," I rattled on enthusiastically. "Do you know that disposable diapers never decompose? Five thousand years from now, this earth is going to be covered with a mile-thick layer of plastic diapers. That's gross. I'm glad we use cloth diapers for the twins."

"I try to be as environmentally conscious as possible," Mom said meekly.

"We could be even more," I said, jumping down from one counter and climbing on another. I waved my sponge in the air as I began telling her of all the ways we could save energy that I had learned at the center.

"First of all, we should get rid of *all* of our spray cans. We can use pump sprayers instead. *And*, we should separate our garbage. I'll take it to the center. We could have a box each for cans, glass, plastic bottles, and paper. And of course we should turn off the lights as much as possible.''

I saw our house as a model for environmental protection. Maybe the newspaper would even do an article about us — about me! I could wear my black-and-white jumper with the red roses on the collar. I've heard that contrasting colors show up well in photographs.

You're being selfish, I reminded myself. With a bang I brought my thoughts back to what was happening then, not to what might happen in the future.

I picked up the cleanser and read the label before I resumed scrubbing. ''Then I was thinking about using biodegradable soap for our dishes and laundry, even for our baths. We could use the wastewater to water our outdoor plants. Think of how much we could conserve!''

I couldn't tell whether Mom was really interested or just being polite, but she listened to everything I had to say. The more I thought about it, the more ideas I had for recycling in our own home. I couldn't wait to get started.

''When do you think we could begin recycling, Mom?'' I asked when I finished wiping the last cupboard.

''Gosh, I don't know exactly,'' Mom said. ''We'll have to talk over some of your ideas with your father. Right now I hear the twins calling me, so I'd better run before they get too upset."

"But, Mom — "

"Thanks for helping me with the cupboards, Steph. I'm glad we got to spend some time together, and I'm going to love opening these cupboards in the morning."

"You're welcome, Mom," I said as she gave me a hug on her way out of the kitchen.

"You'd better get on with your homework."

"I will," I called after her. "Just as soon as I go through our books to see which ones we want to donate to the Library Book Sale."

Feeling pretty satisfied with my day's work, I went to the bookshelves to pick out some books. Being nice took up a lot of time, I thought as I started reading the titles. It was almost nine o'clock and I still hadn't done my homework. The library drive was very important, I told myself. They were counting on me. I had to do that first.

By the time I finished filling a cardboard box with books to give away, it was almost ten o'clock.

"Hadn't you better be going to bed?" Dad said when he walked by the study and saw me still up.

"I will," I said sleepily, "but I still have to finish my math and science and copy over a final draft of a book report."

"It seems to me that you should have done your

homework earlier," Dad remarked. "Ten o'clock is too late to stay up on a weeknight."

"Mrs. Mead will give me a zero if I don't turn in my homework," I told him. "Please, Dad. Just this once, let me stay up and finish it. I promise I'll organize my time better tomorrow night." I sounded almost as whiny as a six-year-old.

"Just this once," Dad said, smoothing my hair back from my forehead. "But don't make a habit of it."

Chapter
5

The next morning was the pits. The music on my red-and-black radio-alarm clock blared for at least five minutes before I heard it. Then, when I was squeezing the toothpaste out, a big blob fell on my pants.

I had to change my whole outfit and by that time I didn't even care what I looked like. I threw on an old, green T-shirt dress — something I hardly ever wear — and stumbled into the kitchen.

I gulped down a glass of milk for breakfast and grabbed my backpack, but I was still running late to meet the others at the corner of Hillcrest and Pine. My shoulders were already aching with the heavy load of library leaflets that I was carrying along with my books.

I hoped I could keep my eyes open long enough to ride to school and stay awake in class.

"Hard night, Stephanie?" Kate asked the minute I raced up.

I was determined not to be grumpy. What good would one day of niceness do if the next day I acted like a bear?

"Nope," I answered her, making myself smile. "I'm in great shape this morning. Isn't it a lovely spring day?" I added, not bothering to look at the sky or notice the weather. "It's so good to be alive!"

"Stephanie, it looks like rain," Lauren said, pointing to the sky.

"Rain is beautiful, too," I said, refusing to be in a bad mood.

"Patti looks like she has a raincloud over her head, too," Kate remarked as Patti joined us. She *did* look like one of those cartoon characters with a little black raincloud following her around.

Lauren was right. It was a totally depressing morning. I wanted to go home, crawl back into bed, and not come out for a week.

STOP!

I couldn't let myself feel this way. Nice people never got depressed. (Even if they were wearing the grossest thing in their closet.) Or at least, if they did, they didn't let their feelings show. My job as a nice person was to make Patti feel better.

"What's wrong, Patti?" Lauren asked. "You look awful!"

"Not awful," I said quickly. "You look just as pretty as ever, but you look kind of sad."

"Is this about the parent-teacher conference? Why didn't you call one of us last night to tell us how it went?" Kate wanted to know.

Patti heaved a big sigh. "I was too upset."

"Why?" I asked. "We'll do everything we can to help."

"Remember when I got into the Quarks, and I thought you guys might not want to be friends with such a dorky science brain?" Patti asked sadly. Quarks is a science club for smart kids in our school.

We all nodded.

"Well, how do you feel about being friends with a sixth-grader?"

I was stunned. Why hadn't I suspected that before? Jenny had been bragging about the possibility for the past two days. And Patti was much smarter than old Jenny Carlin. Of course they wanted to skip her up to the next grade!

"What are you going to do?" Lauren asked.

"This can't be happening!" Kate said.

I couldn't think of anything nice to say, so I didn't say anything at all.

"C'mon," Patti said. "There isn't time to talk about it now. We're going to be late for school if we don't hurry."

"Promise you'll tell us the whole story at recess," I said finally. "There has to be something we can do."

As it turned out, Patti had to stay in at recess for a talk with Mrs. Mead and the principal, Mrs. Wainwright.

Lunch was our first chance to hear her news.

"So, spill it," Kate prompted. "What happened at your conference?"

Patti immediately looked as if she were going to cry. "This is the most terrible thing that has ever happened to me," Patti said. "Mrs. Mead and Mrs. Wainwright want me to skip into sixth grade because my test scores are so high, just like they skipped Horace up to second grade." Horace is Patti's little brother. "My parents think it's a good idea. You know, they've been considering moving me up for months. Now it looks as if it's going to happen. I don't want to leave all my friends!"

"Are you positive?" I asked. "I mean, have they signed official papers and everything?"

"I don't know if they've done that yet," Patti said. "But I'm supposed to start visiting the sixth-grade class tomorrow to see what it's like. That's what Mrs. Mead told me at recess."

"That's bad," Lauren said.

Patti pushed her food around on her tray. "I know. It's like I don't have anything to say about the decision. All the grown-ups have made it for me."

"What do *you* want to do?" I asked, trying not to let it show how much I would miss her. "Are you sure you don't want to go? Maybe you'll like it in sixth grade after you visit and see what it's like."

"No, I won't!" Patti said. "I'll feel like a baby."

"Don't worry. We'll get you out of this somehow," Lauren promised.

Kate finished off her lunch and pushed the tray aside. "Yeah, we'll be rid of Jenny Carlin, but we'll figure out a way to keep you in 5B."

Patti leaned forward. "I have some other news," she said. "I overheard part of Jenny's conference because it was right before mine. She *didn't* get invited to skip into sixth grade."

"You're kidding!" Kate whispered, leaning in closer. "She was so sure she would."

"Mrs. Mead told her parents that Jenny's *scores* are high enough, but her grades don't match. She's not working up to her potential, so they don't think she's ready to handle the extra work of sixth grade," Patti confided.

Just then Jenny and Angela walked by our table. *Stomped* by was a better description. The thunderous expression on Jenny's face made Patti's little raincloud look like a puff of cotton.

Lauren and Kate hid their grins behind their hands. A couple of giggles escaped. I kicked Kate under the table to try to keep her from laughing out loud.

Jenny whirled around and slammed her tray in front of us on our table. "So you heard? So what!"

It was all I could do to keep from laughing myself. Jenny Carlin taken down a peg! She was always being so mean and snobby to everyone else. She deserved a little of her own medicine.

I started to come back at her with one of her own lines about maturity —

Be nice. Be nice. Be nice, I repeated to myself like a broken record in my head.

"Oh, that's too bad, Jenny," I managed to choke out. "I know what it's like to feel really disappointed about something."

Lauren and Kate raised their eyebrows in perfect synchronization. Then they both coughed, trying to keep from laughing.

"Try your sticky-sweet act on someone else!" Jenny snubbed me. "What's it to you, anyway?"

No gratitude at all, I thought. I felt my eyes narrow and my eyebrows draw together in a scowl. A lot of good it does me to try to be nice! Jenny doesn't deserve sympathy. She deserves a kick in the shins!

But I wasn't going to say anything. I wasn't going to get hooked into an argument. That's what Jenny wanted, and I wasn't going to give her the satisfaction.

"Excuse me," I said, standing up. "I want to get some fresh air before going back to class."

Then I walked away. I slid my tray through the dishwasher's window and walked out the door into the playground. I didn't look back to see the expressions on anyone's face. I had to get out of there or I knew I would say something — something I would later regret.

Being wonderful was a hard, thankless job. I wondered if it got easier with more practice. I sure hoped so.

There was one bright spot in my day, however. Mrs. Mead let me give a speech in class that afternoon about saving the library. I passed out the leaflets. Thank goodness. They were so heavy! I had permanent grooves worn in my shoulders from lugging them around in my backpack.

"The library needs as many volunteers as it can get," I told the class enthusiastically. "It's really an easy job. All you have to do is pass out forms to your neighbors and then go back a few days later to collect the books and pledges. The library is an important part of our community," I went on. "It's important for our education as well as for the pleasure of reading. If anyone would like to take a few extra leaflets, I'll be happy to give them to you."

They didn't know how happy!

Five people raised their hands for more leaflets. Karla Stamos was one of them. *Figures,* I thought to myself. *Karla is the biggest grind in class.*

Then I instantly felt ashamed of my mean thought. I gave Karla a big smile as I handed her a stack of leaflets. "Just stop by the library and sign up on the volunteer list," I explained. "If anyone has any questions, just call me at home. My number is 555–2478."

Despite my efforts at niceness, I hoped Karla didn't call me. I wasn't sure how nice I would be if she did.

"Thank you, Stephanie," Mrs. Mead said after I sat down. "It's good to see our students here at Riverhurst becoming involved with the community on a greater scale. Volunteer work is a great way to make new friends and help a worthy cause. More people should follow your example."

I felt really great. Still, when I met eyes with Lauren, Kate, and Patti, I saw some confusion in their faces. I hoped they realized I was doing it all for them.

Chapter
6

Patti looked even sadder when she rode up to the corner of Hillcrest and Pine the next morning. We were the first two there. I had made a special effort to get up earlier and try to wear something decent to school, but I didn't really care that much about my red stretch-pants and matching T-shirt at that moment.

I was more concerned with Patti. "What's wrong?" I asked as soon as she stopped.

"I have to spend half of the afternoon in the sixth-grade classroom today," she announced. She looked ready to cry.

I knew my "it's a beautiful day" comment was not going to work on her that morning.

"I'm really sorry," I told her. "Are you scared? I know I would be." I tried to empathize with her. Empathize means to put yourself in another person's shoes — try to feel what they feel. I had learned that in one of my books on friendship.

"I'm more embarrassed than scared. The sixth-graders are all going to make fun of me. I won't have any friends. I don't care how smart I am, I'm going to be behind and playing catch-up because I'm coming into the class late. Now I *really* know how Horace felt!" Horace had had some rough days when he skipped a grade.

I put the kickstand down on my bike and walked over to where Patti was still straddling hers. I had to think of a way to cheer her up.

"Maybe it won't be as bad as you think," I said.

"Name one thing that will be good," Patti challenged.

"Well, for one thing, you're as tall or taller than most of the kids. You won't stick out in the crowd like Kate or I would," I told her.

"Name another thing," Patti said.

I thought hard. "You already *do* have lots of friends in the sixth grade. Some are your friends from Quarks, and some we just know from going to school with them. Sixth-graders aren't some kind of monsters. Besides," I added, "they were all fifth-graders last year."

"Very funny." Patti smiled slightly. "And they were fourth-graders the year before."

"And kindergartners four years before that.

Now, you aren't afraid of kindergartners, are you?''

Patti's smile grew. "I guess when you put it that way, they aren't that different from me.''

"Some of them probably aren't even a whole year older than us," I reminded her. "Your visit will only be for two hours. You'll do fine. After school you can tell us all of the terrible, horrible things that happened.''

Patti's lips turned down into a frown again. "But what happens when I have to stay there all day? I'm going to hate it. I know I will.''

"Look," I told her. "There's no point in worrying about it before it actually happens. Until then, just pretend your afternoon visits are a vacation from 5B. I wouldn't mind getting out of class for a couple of hours myself. Want me to take your place?''

My offer made her smile again. "Thanks," she said. "You make it sound so easy, Steph. I'm not so scared now that I know it's just a vacation.''

It wasn't until later on that morning that I realized I had done something nice without even planning to! But Patti made it easy to be nice. She had needed someone to talk to, and I was there. It was simple. The Sleepover Friends are always there for each other.

I started thinking about people who didn't have a friend to talk to when they needed it. Karla Stamos was a good example. Hardly anyone ever talked to her. No one ever invited her to be with them on their group projects. Mrs. Mead always had to assign her to a group. And no one ever sat with her at lunch.

How sad, I thought as I walked past Karla on my way to our regular table at lunch. There she was, sitting by herself, looking super lonely.

My friends could do without me for one lunch period. Karla needed a friend. As part of my niceness plan, I decided to sit with her and keep her company. I smiled, imagining how grateful she would be to have me join her for lunch.

I tried to ignore the looks of astonishment on my friends' faces when I detoured to Karla's table. I knew it was a risk to my reputation, but I had to do it. Nice people did what was right, no matter what.

"Hi, Karla," I said as I came up to her table. "Mind if I join you?"

"Whatever," Karla grunted.

"So . . . how have you been lately?" I started the conversation.

"Fine."

I took a bite of a carrot stick. "Me, too," I said, when she didn't say anything else. "How's school going?"

"Fine."

This was harder than I thought. I was getting nowhere fast. Karla didn't even look up from her food. She didn't appear to be grateful at all that I had stopped by her table. But I couldn't leave without giving it one more try.

A nice person would try to find something that Karla was interested in and get her talking about it. I thought for a minute.

It wouldn't be boys. Karla barely talked to the girls, much less the boys. She didn't belong to any clubs that I knew of, or participate in any sports. And she hadn't started collecting for the library yet. Let's face it — Karla was pretty boring.

The longer the silence between us dragged out, the more boring lunch became, too. Finally I hit on homework. Everyone had something to say about Mrs. Mead's homework. She gave the most homework in the whole school.

"Boy," I began again. "Wasn't that science homework terrible last night? It took me two whole hours!"

"But it was very interesting, don't you think?" Karla said, perking up. "I mean, learning about all of those parasites was fascinating. Did you read about the planarian? Or the flatworm that can regenerate lost parts? Or about how the earthworm uses its bristles to cling to the walls of a tunnel?"

"Tell me about it," I invited, feeling grossed out, but very pleased with myself for finding a subject that Karla enjoyed.

Ten minutes later I wasn't smiling. In fact, it was all I could do not to fall asleep! And Karla was still talking. I didn't know how much longer I could stand listening to her elaborate on the exoskeleton of the arthropod, whatever that was!

I really wanted to be sitting at my regular table with my regular friends. I had seen a really cute necklace in Just Juniors that I wanted to tell them about. I thought maybe we could all get ones to match.

In the background I could hear their laughter. Lunchtime was usually our special time to gossip and catch up on the news from the day before. Instead of being there and finding out what was going on in my best friends' lives, I was being a nice person by sitting and listening to Karla drone on about the science homework. I spent so much time with Karla that there was no time to talk to the others before we went back to class.

Sometimes being wonderful is the pits.

All afternoon I kept glancing at Patti's empty seat and feeling sad. It really would be awful if Patti left us permanently. It wouldn't just be the rest of the year in fifth grade, either. I mean, when we went into sixth, Patti wouldn't even go to Riverhurst Elementary anymore. She'd be at the junior high! She'd always be a year ahead for the rest of school. She was bound to find new friends — and then where would that leave us?

Suddenly I felt very sorry that I had spent what might be one of our last lunches together eating with Karla Stamos. Patti was much more important to me. I would be sure to make it up to her that afternoon.

Then I remembered Hope and the recycling center. It was supposed to be my first day working there on a regular basis. I couldn't let Hope down, either. My life was starting to get very complicated.

After school Hope and I rode off on our bikes to the RRC. Patti had to stay after school again, so none of us were able to talk to her.

Once we arrived at the recycling center, I resolved to put my worries about Patti in the back of my mind. I wanted to learn all there was to know about recycling.

The people at the center were happy to tell me — about all the trees killed to make paper, how bad Styrofoam is for the environment, the oil spill crisis, the ozone layer, air pollution, water pollution, fish with poisonous mercury in them. By the time I finished listening to their stories, I knew how desperate the situation was.

I felt incredibly depressed. I'd had no idea the world was in such bad shape.

I have to do something about it, I thought as I

helped Hope fold and staple the center's newsletter (printed on recycled paper, of course). Something more than just sending out a newsletter.

Hundreds of newsletters later, my arm and hand were aching from pressing the stapler, and my hands were full of paper cuts. The lack of sleep from the last two nights must have been catching up with me, too, because I felt like taking a nap right there on the finished stack.

From four-thirty until five o'clock I watched the minute hand creep around the clock until it was time to go. I was kind of surprised that good people get bored, too — even when they're doing something important.

"See you girls next Tuesday," Barbara called after us as we headed toward home on our bikes.

"Well, how did you like it?" Hope asked as we rode along.

"I learned a lot," I told her truthfully. "And the work was . . . very fulfilling." That was another word I had read in one of my niceness books. It meant that a person felt satisfied and good after doing something worthwhile.

I didn't tell her that I also felt worn out. My head was pounding from taking in so much information and trying to figure out what to do with it.

There was *one* thing I was sure of. I would have to do something more about the recycling crisis. Jeffrey had talked about the local restaurants and businesses that had no plans to recycle. If I didn't try to convince them to do it, who would?

As soon as I got some sleep I was going to tell Lauren, Kate, and Patti about some of my ideas for making Riverhurst a model recycling community. I was sure they would be as excited about it as me — after all, they're three of the nicest people I know.

As soon as I got some sleep.

Chapter
7

I was too tired even to call Patti when I got home. I helped Dad with the dishes, did my homework, and rolled into bed at about eight o'clock. That was an hour and a half earlier than I usually went to bed, but I didn't care.

The next morning I overslept and Mom had to drive me to school with my bike in the trunk. At lunch I made sure to sit with my friends so that I could hear about Patti's visit to sixth grade.

"I felt like a little kid," Patti said the minute we sat down with our lunches. "The topics that Mrs. Langhorn talked about were harder than we have now, but interesting. Still, I felt out of place."

"Of course you did," Lauren sympathized. "I think your parents should reconsider this move. Parents shouldn't force you to do things that make you miserable."

"Are you kidding?" Kate said. "Parents do that all the time."

"How would you know?" I asked. "You have great parents."

"I know. But sometimes they have the weirdest ideas about what I should be doing and when. I mean, I'll be sitting there doing my homework and Mom will suddenly remember that I haven't cleaned my room or taken out the trash in a week. She expects me to jump up right that minute, in the middle of reading a chapter, and do what she says."

"That's not the same as Patti, though," I said. "Skipping into sixth grade is a lot different from taking out the trash."

"Don't worry, Patti," Lauren said. "Tonight at the sleepover we'll come up with a plan. That is, of course, if Kate can take a break from her oh-so-many chores."

"*Very* funny!" Kate said, then started laughing. "Okay, so maybe I exaggerated a little. But you should see what Melissa gets away with. Mom still cleans her room for her! And she has *never* taken out the trash in her life. It's disgusting!"

"She's only eight," I said, giggling. "Give the kid a break!"

"Weren't you taking out the trash when you were eight?" Kate shot back.

"Well . . . I guess I was. I see what you mean. It must make a difference whether you're the oldest or the youngest."

"*So there!*" Kate declared. "We ought to ask Lauren how many chores she has to do compared to her big brother Roger."

"Wait a minute!" Lauren said, pretending to protect herself with her hands. "I may be messy, but I've taken out the trash a few times in my life!"

I shook my head, smiling. It was fun laughing and talking with my friends again. I had been so busy lately that two days ago seemed like forever. "Speaking of trash, Kate," I said, thinking about my plan to involve them in a recycling project.

"What about it?" Kate asked suspiciously, her smile wavering.

"Well, you know Hope and I worked at the recycling center yesterday," I reminded them. "We found out that most of the local restaurants and stores have no plans to recycle anything. Can you imagine how many tons of aluminum, glass, and paper are thrown away each day in Riverhurst?"

"A lot, I suppose," Patti said. "But what can we do about it?"

I grinned. It was good to see Patti's mind concentrating on something other than sixth grade.

"Glad you asked," I said. "One of the names

on the list of places that don't recycle is the Pizza Palace at the mall!" The Pizza Palace is one of our very favorite places to eat.

"The Pizza Palace!" Kate said thoughtfully. "They must throw away tons of cardboard boxes."

"Not to mention all the soda cans and plastic forks and knives," Patti said.

"We have to do something about it!" I said, standing up and leaning forward on the table. "Recycling is one of the most important things we can do to save the planet. We have to at least try if we're going to keep living on earth!"

"Steph — where else would we live?" Lauren muttered.

"What's going on?" Hope asked as she walked over and joined us. "Are you practicing a speech, Stephanie?"

"I was telling them about the Pizza Palace and the other restaurants that aren't recycling," I told her. "We can't just sit here and watch the earth disappear, one pizza box at a time. Do you have any ideas?" I asked her eagerly.

"Why don't we talk to John, the manager at the Pizza Palace? Maybe we could offer to help him get started?" Hope suggested.

"John is really nice," Patti mentioned. "I'm sure if we explained how important it is to recycle, he would be willing to start a program."

Kate pulled out her notebook and started writing down suggestions. Even Lauren joined in. She was particularly interested in the idea that John might give us pizza as a reward for setting him on the recycling track. Natch! Her name should be Lauren Hunger! That was one of our old jokes.

Lunch period flew by. Patti perked up as we worked out ideas for making local store owners aware of the need for recycling.

"Maybe the Quarks could make some posters to put up in community display cases at the mall," Patti suggested.

"Cool," I said. "Kind of like the displays at the recycling center."

"That might be really effective," Hope agreed, and Kate wrote it down.

I was really happy. This is how I thought it would be when I started my niceness plan. Everyone was beginning to notice that I was accomplishing good things. People were beginning to think of me as a good person, a nice person.

Soon I wouldn't have to worry at all about losing my Sleepover Friends. Not only that, everyone else would want to be my friend, too.

I tuned out of the conversation for a minute, imagining what it would be like to be crowned "Most Popular Friend in the World."

Swirls of white mist parted before my mind's eye

and I saw myself surrounded by happy people, all asking for my autograph.

"How does it feel to be so nice that everyone wants to be your friend?" the imaginary television reporter asked me.

I took the microphone from her with a smile. "I haven't done anything special," I told her modestly. "I've just lived by the motto, 'Think of others first, and each day try to make the world a better place.' "

A hush fell over the crowd as they thought about my profound words. I touched the silk banner on my shoulder and smiled for the camera as they all broke into a thunderous round of applause. . . .

"Steph!" I heard Kate's voice over the roar of the crowd.

"She's daydreaming," Lauren said. "Probably thinking about the three thousand tons of aluminum she can personally save from the garbage dump."

"More likely she's thinking about stopping off at Just Juniors on the way to the Pizza Palace," Kate said.

"Sorry," I told them, still glowing from my imaginary interview. "Let's talk more about it at the sleepover tonight, okay?"

"Whatever you say," Kate scoffed. "Just try to stay on the planet, would you?"

"Ha-ha!" I said laughing. "*Veerry* funny!"

Later that afternoon, before it was time to go to

Kate's house for the sleepover, I helped my mom clean the whole house. I did the bathrooms while she did dishes and mopped the kitchen floor. While the twins slept I vacuumed the living room and dusted all the windowsills.

I finished folding two loads of laundry and walked into the kitchen to find Mom staring into the open refrigerator. "I don't have any idea what to fix for dinner tonight, Steph."

"The kitchen is so clean, Mom. It's a shame to mess it up again by cooking," I said, looking around at the shining counters. Feeding Emma and Jeremy would destroy the freshly waxed floor.

Mom shut the refrigerator and opened a cupboard. She scanned the rows of canned goods.

"I know," I said. "Let's go out for pizza!"

"You know, that's a good idea, Stephanie. We deserve a break after all this work," Mom said, shutting the cupboard. Then she started rummaging around in the drawer next to the stove. "Don't we have some half-price coupons around here for the Pizza Palace?"

"May we invite Lauren, Kate, and Patti?" I asked. "We wanted to talk to John, the manager, about recycling, anyway."

"Here they are!" Mom said, triumphantly holding up the coupons. "Of course you can invite them. Why don't you give them a call right now? And while you're on the phone with the Hunters, I'll try to get Mrs. Campbell from next door to baby-sit the twins while we go."

Just like old times, I thought later as we dug into the Pizza Palace's thick-crust, combination pizza. Me and my friends out to dinner with my parents on a sleepover night — and no twins.

Mom said exactly what I was thinking. "It sure is peaceful without the twins along for a change. Isn't it, Ron?"

"We ought to go out like this more often," he agreed, smiling at Mom, then at the rest of us.

After dinner, Patti, Lauren, Kate, and I squared our shoulders and marched together to the counter to talk to John. Suddenly I was worried about what he might say. What if he threw us out?

John was nice. He wouldn't do that. Would he?

Everyone waited for me to approach him. A feeling of panic rose in my throat and I wondered if I would be able to speak — which is pretty unusual for me! Then I remembered that after I had swallowed my fear, I had successfully gotten library pledges. I could do this, too!

"Uh, hi, John," I said. "Do you have a minute to talk to us?"

"Sure! You girls ready to take on another pizza? I'll order it right up for you."

"No, that's not it. We wanted to talk to you about recycling."

"Oh, recycling, is it?" he said. "Well, what about it? Are you collecting cans for a school project or something?"

"Not exactly," I told him. "I've been working at the Riverhurst Recycling Center, and I found out that your restaurant doesn't have any plans to recycle. We were hoping we could make you change your mind."

"Recycling is important," John agreed. "But it's not cost-effective. Do you know what that means?"

We shook our heads.

"It means that it would cost me more to recycle than the recycling would pay back. Besides, my employees and I don't have enough time to separate everything and take it to the recycling center."

"But it wouldn't be that big a deal," Kate said. "You could have three different garbage cans and train your people to just toss the pizza boxes into one, the cans into another, and the food garbage into the third."

"How much time could that take?" Lauren asked.

"Believe it or not, too much," John said. "Now, I'd really like to help you girls out, but it's just not possible. Thanks for being concerned, though."

"I guess that means he's not going to do it," I said later as my parents drove us back to Pine Street. I felt really disappointed. I had been thinking, *Today the Pizza Palace, tomorrow the world*, but we were stopped before we even got started.

"Yeah, it's too bad, but what can we do about it?" Kate asked.

"I don't know," I said, "but I'm going to think of something."

We drove past Donald Foster's house and turned into the driveway at Number 7 Pine. It was hard to look at the house down the street, Number 11, and not wish that Lauren still lived there. To me, it seemed that the disappointment at the Pizza Palace was spilling over into all of my thoughts. The Pizza Palace, Lauren moving, Patti heading for sixth grade — nothing was going right — and it didn't matter how nice I was being.

Snap out of it! I told myself as we walked up the driveway and into Kate's house. It was time to cheer Patti up about her move to sixth grade.

We said hello to Mr. and Mrs. Beekman, who were watching a movie with Kate's little sister, Melissa, in the family room. Then we filed upstairs to Kate's super-neat room and flopped down on her bed.

"Okay, Patti," I said. "Tell us how you really feel."

So Patti told us about her second visit to the sixth grade that afternoon.

"We broke into groups and no one in my group even talked to me," Patti complained. "They had all been studying different countries and I wanted to tell about my family's trip to Mexico last year."

Patti's parents are both history professors at the local university. The summer before they had taken twenty students to study the ruins in the Yucatán peninsula.

"So what happened?" Lauren asked.

"No one cared about what I had to say. One girl even said that since I hadn't done a twenty-page report like the rest of them had, what I had to say didn't count."

"What a jerk!" Kate said. "Who was it? I'll give her a piece of my mind!"

"Now, it's not necessary to know who it was," I interrupted before Patti had a chance to tell her. "The point is, we have to figure out a way to get Patti out of this mess."

"What if we can't?" Patti asked.

"We'll still see each other at lunch, before and after school, at sleepovers, and on the weekends," Lauren reassured her.

"I'm not even going to see you at lunchtime," Patti wailed. "Mrs. Langhorn's class always has the second lunch period, and Mrs. Mead's has the first."

I saw tears beginning to well up in her eyes.

"Oh, no!" Kate exclaimed. "This is worse than I thought."

Suddenly Patti jumped up and ran off to the bathroom to get a tissue. The three of us sat in a circle looking at each other.

"We can't let them take her away," Kate finally said.

"What if some of her new friends begin asking her to their own sleepovers?" Lauren said worriedly. "She'll have more in common with them. We could end up losing Patti for good!"

"All I know," I said, "is that we have to do our best to keep Patti's mind off of her troubles tonight. Aren't you guys hungry for dessert yet?"

"Right," Lauren said, getting my meaning. "As soon as Patti comes out of the bathroom, we'll head for the kitchen and whip up a wild dessert."

"Then we'll play some wild games," Kate said, grinning at me. "Our usual: Mad Libs, Truth or Dare . . ."

"Whatever it takes," I vowed.

Chapter 8

The dessert distraction worked well. Mrs. Beekman had made a batch of giant cookies — sweetened with applesauce for Lauren — and we decided to decorate them with reduced-sugar whipped cream, chopped nuts, and dried fruit pieces. Patti was so busy trying out new designs on her cookie that she forgot (almost) about sixth grade.

We were sitting at the kitchen table, trying to outdo each other's decorations, when Kate's sister Melissa showed up wanting a snack.

A few months ago, Kate would have immediately thrown a fit and kicked her out of the kitchen, but they had been getting along better lately. Tonight she pulled out a chair and handed Melissa a cookie. She didn't talk to her, though. That was probably asking too much!

"How was school today?" I asked Melissa. "Did

you explode any more volcanoes in science class?"

Melissa grinned. "Nope. We made a color wheel and spun it to mix the colors. It was neat."

I helped Melissa spread some whipped cream on her cookie and showed her how to make a face with nuts and sunflower seeds.

"What colors did you use?"

"Red and yellow to make orange, blue and red to make purple, and yellow and blue to make green. Want to see?" Melissa asked.

"Sure, I'd love to," I told her sincerely. "We all would."

Melissa ran to the counter to get her science folder, and I sat back in my chair and smiled. Being nice was easy. People really responded. More people had smiled at me during the past week than in the past year.

I must be doing something right.

Of course I had to ignore the strange looks that Lauren, Kate, and Patti exchanged while I was exclaiming over Melissa's science project. I could tell she enjoyed all the attention I was giving her.

"Melissa! Time for bed," Mrs. Beekman called.

"Thanks for showing it to me," I told Melissa a few moments later. "Have a nice sleep."

Kate felt my forehead the minute that Melissa left the room. "You're not going to start hanging around with my little sister again, are you?" Kate asked.

"No way!" I said.

Everybody laughed. They remembered the last time I had befriended Melissa. It hadn't turned out so well.

Kate still had her hand on my forehead. She bent over to look into my eyes. "She feels normal. She looks normal. I don't know what's wrong," she told the others.

I slapped her hand away playfully. "Are you a doctor now?" I teased.

"I wish I were a psychologist. You've been acting very strange lately," Kate pronounced.

Lauren nodded, but Patti just smiled.

"I think Stephanie has been acting very nice lately," Patti said.

"*Too* nice," Kate remarked.

"Well, I'm ready to play some games," I said, changing the subject.

"Truth or Dare," Kate announced. "Let's go get comfortable in my room."

"First let's make some popcorn," Lauren said.

Everyone looked at her as if she were crazy.

Lauren shrugged her shoulders. "I know we're full now, but we might get hungry later during the movie."

We all groaned. Lauren Hunger strikes again!

Lugging a huge bowl of popcorn and a two-liter bottle of diet Dr Pepper, we trooped off to Kate's room.

"I didn't ask before, but is that a new poster of *Gone With the Wind*?" I asked Kate.

"It's cool, isn't it?" Kate said, smoothing the corner down. "Aunt Lela sent it from Medford. She went to a Clark Gable film festival. See, it's signed by the artist. My dad says I can have it framed."

"Fancy," Patti said. "I'd like to get some of my animal posters framed. I saw some cheap poster frames down at Hale's Hobby and Craft Shop in the mall."

"We should go down tomorrow and take a look at them," Kate said.

I didn't say anything. I knew I was going to be busy doing my volunteer work on Saturday. I had to pass out more leaflets and collect books for the library. I was also thinking of donating some time to the Sea Mammal League. They save whales and porpoises that wash up on the beach, and go to areas to clean up after oil spills and stuff.

I had read in the newspaper that they needed volunteers, so I thought it might be nice for me to do it. I'd wait until tomorrow to tell Lauren, Kate, and Patti about that, though.

"Who wants to go first?" Lauren asked.

"Me," I said. "Patti, truth or dare?"

"Um, truth," Patti said, leaning back on one elbow.

"Describe the most romantic date that you could go on and who you would go with."

Patti blushed. "Do I have to answer?"

"Of course," I said, pretending to be stern.

"Well, um — uh — I guess I'd go with Henry Larkin," Patti said quietly.

"Well, of course she would," Kate said. "No surprise. Everyone knows they're almost engaged. That question was too easy."

Patti and Henry had practically announced to the world that they liked each other when they had danced together at the Valentine's Day dance.

"Go on, Patti," I said, putting my finger in front of my lips and shushing Kate. "What would you guys do?" I asked with a grin. I have to admit it — I can think up the *best* Truth or Dare questions.

Patti gazed at the ceiling. "I think it would be really romantic if Henry packed a picnic lunch and took me to the lake. We'd find a quiet spot, and he would lay out a checkered tablecloth complete with flowers in a vase and fancy dishes. We would eat all our favorite foods, then gaze at the clouds together until our stomachs settled enough to go swimming. Then we would go home."

"Don't you even want him to kiss you?" Lauren asked.

"Ew!" Kate said, wrinkling her nose and laughing.

Patti blushed again. "I answered the question already. No more details."

"Whoa!" Kate whooped. "Patti and Henry, sitting in a tree — K-I-S-S-I-N-G . . ."

"Shut up!" Patti screeched, giggling and throwing a pillow at Kate.

Of course we all had to grab our pillows and slam them into each other for a few minutes.

When we had calmed down, it was Patti's turn. She chose Lauren, and Lauren chose dare. Patti dared her to call up Ginger Kinkaid and say she was the butcher delivering her order of pickled pig's feet. It worked like a charm. Lauren used a deep, gruff voice and spoke through a handkerchief.

When Ginger said, "What? I don't need pig's feet!" Lauren said, "That's because you already have them!"

Everyone roared with laughter except me. I had a hard time not cracking a smile, of course, but I didn't think that a nice person would think it was funny.

When Lauren asked me, I chose truth. I didn't want to have to make a joke phone call to some innocent person.

"If there were three people you could order to move out of town, who would they be and why?" Lauren asked.

Wow — this was a tough one! Can a nice person ever admit that they want some people to move out of town?

I thought about Ginger and Jenny and Karla. This was a terrible question because it meant I had to put down some people. No matter how much they deserved it, it wasn't on my niceness plan.

"May I have another question?" I asked politely.

"Nope."

"Well, it's just that I wouldn't want to order *anyone* out of town," I said. "Even Ginger Kinkaid. As rotten and snobby as she is, she has her good points. And she has been awfully upset since her parents decided to get a divorce. And Karla can't help it if she's quiet and boring. She can't help it if she has no taste in clothes. If more people tried to be her friend, she would probably act differently. And of course Jenny is simply disappointed by her — "

"Stop! Stop! I've heard enough." Kate jumped up and stared at me. "What is wrong with you, Stephanie?"

"I don't know what you're talking about!" I said.

"Don't you? You haven't been yourself for a week now. We can't even gossip about people or have a really embarrassing game of Truth or Dare because you're too busy defending everyone's honor."

"Sorry!" I said hotly. Then I quickly shut up and sat there clenching my fists and trying to calm down.

Why was Kate mad at me? I wondered. I thought my being nice was supposed to make everyone like me more! Now Kate was mad because I was being nice instead of cutting everyone down behind their backs like I usually did. It didn't make sense! I couldn't please her no matter what I did!

It seemed as if I couldn't please *anyone*. Lauren started in on me next. "Yeah, and I'd like to know why you're doing so much volunteer work?" she asked curiously. "Are you running for Congress or something?"

"I'm not running for anything," I said. Except maybe for "best friend of the year" award. "I just enjoy helping out a good cause."

My lower lip started to tremble and I bit it. I felt like my friends were attacking me. It wasn't fair!

"There's more to it than that," Kate declared. "Sooner or later we're going to find out what brought all this on." She raised her eyebrows significantly and left the room.

The rest of the evening went okay. When Kate came back a few minutes later, we had all calmed down. We sat in a circle on her bed to talk about all the stuff going on at school.

I tried to tone down my positive comments so that Kate wouldn't jump on me again. I just made sure that I wasn't the one who started any gossip. I also offered to turn the lights off when everyone was in bed, and helped Patti unstick the zipper on her sleeping bag when it got stuck. It was the least I could do.

The next morning I was exhausted from trying to be nice and thinking about being nice, then worrying all night whether I had been *too* nice. I wasn't sure I could keep up this pace!

After breakfast of hash browns and eggs, à la Mr. Beekman, who's a great cook, we all began to pack up our things.

"Let's go to the mall today and check out that frame shop," Lauren suggested.

"Okay," Patti said.

Patti and Lauren went to call their parents. When they came back and I was still standing there, Kate asked, "What's the matter? Do you have other plans again?"

"Well . . ." I hesitated. What Kate had said last night still bothered me. "I thought I might go over to the Sea Mammal League to see if they need any weekend volunteers. It feels great to give yourself to a cause. Why don't you guys come, too?'' Somehow I didn't sound that convincing, even to myself.

"I don't think so,'' Kate said, frowning. "Besides, I thought shopping was your cause.''

"I can shop anytime,'' I said. "Why don't you go on — and then we can meet later and plan our campaign to convince the Pizza Palace to start recycling. We could make some posters and put them on sandwich boards. Or maybe even organize a picket line!'' I was beginning to get excited again. I had some great ideas!

Lauren started zipping up her backpack. Patti was looking at the ceiling, probably remembering her imaginary date with Henry Larkin.

Kate looked ready to explode.

"No, thanks,'' she said tightly. "I think I'd rather spend my Saturday having fun at the mall.''

"You do whatever you want, Steph,'' Lauren finally said. "We'll call you later. If you can spare some time for us then, just let us know.''

"Bye,'' Patti said. "Have a good day.''

I frowned, feeling confused.

How good a day was it going to be without my Sleepover Friends?

Chapter 9

The people at the Sea Mammal League were happy to sign me up for a few hours of work on Saturday. Being a fifth-grader, my work was about the same as it had been at the recycling center and the library. I couldn't work directly on fund-raising or run any machinery. Instead, I folded, stapled, and mailed. I was in a room by myself while all the older volunteers spent their time in the phone room, making calls to ask for donations.

The whole time I was there I kept thinking about the mall. I wished I were shopping with my friends. I wished I were checking out the poster frames in the frame shop. Volunteering isn't very much fun by yourself.

Then I felt guilty. Volunteering wasn't supposed to be *fun*. It was supposed to be *nice*. I shouldn't care whether there was anyone there to notice me.

The value was in doing something unselfishly. Right?

I gave myself a little talking to. "Stephanie Green," I said to myself as I lugged a heavy box of sealed envelopes across the room, "you aren't a very nice person. These people need you — not to mention those sea mammals — and all you can think of is escaping to the mall. You should be ashamed of yourself!"

So when the volunteer coordinator, Jack, came in to ask if I would come back the next day, I immediately said I would. I had to prove to myself and to everyone else that I wasn't a quitter.

On Sunday the Sleepover Friends called each other early and agreed to ride our bikes later in the morning to Charlie's. We especially wanted to talk about what to do about Patti's skipping a grade.

We all arrived at almost the same time and, after locking our bikes out front, we went in to find a booth.

"Maybe Patti should start doing badly in school," Lauren suggested. "They wouldn't skip her if her grades dropped."

"That's true," Kate said. "She could also quit going to Quarks. She can say she just doesn't like it anymore."

"I have an idea," I said. "Maybe we can get Horace to tell their parents how miserable he's been since he skipped. Skipping a grade doesn't have to run in the family, does it?"

Patti shook her head and continued to shake it while we gave more suggestions. "Stop!" she said. Then she took a long drink of her milk shake.

"Number one, I don't want to do badly in school. I like getting good grades," she said miserably. "And number two, there's no way I would quit the Quarks. It's too much fun. And number three, Horace isn't unhappy about skipping anymore. He's made new friends and thinks second grade is great."

"We're back to where we started," Kate said with a sigh. "You're not helping us out much, Patti."

"Sorry."

We all sat, sipping our shakes and shaking our heads between sips.

"I know," I said. "We could go to the library!"

"Forget it, Stephanie," Lauren said. "No one is in the mood for more volunteer work."

"That's not what I meant," I said, hurt. "I meant that we could do some research. You know, look up about kids who skip grades and what effect it has on them. Maybe we'll find a book that says it's a horrible thing to do."

"That's a great idea!" Patti said.

Everyone brightened up, but I was upset by Lauren's first reaction. Were my friends still mad at me for giving my time to worthy causes? How could it be? They were the ones who wanted me to improve my niceness quotient in the first place!

They were probably just testing me, I decided. They wanted to see if I would continue to follow through, or if I would quit, proving what a selfish person I really was.

"Yeah, good thinking, Steph," Kate exclaimed. "Let's go as soon as we finish here."

"I'm ready," Lauren said.

"Me, too," Patti echoed.

"Me, three," I said. Then I remembered something. I looked at the clock. "Uh, actually, I can't make it today. . . ."

I had to tell them why. "I promised I'd finish my job at the Sea Mammal League. So I'll call you tonight to see what you found out. Okay, Patti?"

"Yeah, sure," Patti said. But she had a frown on her face. It matched the one on mine as I turned and walked out the door, leaving my friends behind.

The mailing took longer than I thought. It seemed pretty boring, too. I arrived home just before dinner, exhausted, and ready to go to sleep. But after we ate, Mom asked me to help her wash the walls in the bathroom, so of course I did it because a nice person wouldn't say no. *Then* I remembered that I had to do my math homework and read two chapters in my science book for a possible pop quiz on Monday!

I fell asleep somewhere in the middle of arthropod identification. My dreams were of centipedes stapling bulletins with lobsters and shrimp. Spiders kept spinning webs over the boxes, and crayfish had to cut the webs with their claws.

When I woke up the next morning, I felt as if I had worked all night. And I realized I'd forgotten to call Patti the night before.

As we rode our bikes to school, I tried to be cheerful, but didn't quite make it. No one said anything, though. They were too interested in what Patti had found in the books they had checked out of the library. Patti told us about a bunch of statistics on the success rate of kids who skip a grade. I didn't pay much attention because I had a headache from not getting enough sleep.

By lunchtime, though, I felt better and was ready to listen. As soon as we set down our trays on the table, I said, "Could you explain what you found out at the library again, Patti? It was hard to make sense of it when we were riding to school."

"I don't have to tell you all the statistics again," Patti said. "The most important thing I found out was this — that 'skipped' kids sometimes feel out of synch. Their schoolwork and their emotions aren't at the same age," she explained.

"Kind of like what happened to Jenny, but the other way around," I said. *Ooops* — I couldn't help it — it just slipped out! The others cracked up. "Wait — that's not what I meant," I said. "I meant that her emotions aren't as mature as her math skills. I mean . . . her math skills aren't as mature as her mind. . . . Oh, I don't know what I meant. Do you, Patti?"

"Sort of," Patti said, giggling. "Anyway, the book said that the change to a higher grade can make kids insecure, and can have a very traumatic effect on their emotional development."

"Which, in plain English, means you shouldn't do it, right?" Kate said.

"Right," Patti agreed. "I *have* been feeling out of synch since I started visiting Mrs. Langhorn's class last week. Not to mention how much extra work I would have to do to catch up with what her class has done so far this year."

"Do you think your parents will listen to reason?" Lauren asked.

"I'm sure of it," Patti said, confidently patting the book she had just quoted. "But meanwhile, I still have to spend my afternoons in sixth grade."

Suddenly Jenny Carlin laughed loudly behind

us. As usual, she had been eavesdropping on our conversation.

"I can't believe it, Angela," she practically shouted. "Some people are so geeky that they actually don't want to be in the coolest grade in school!"

Henry Larkin turned around from the next table over and smiled at Patti. Then he shook his head and frowned at Jenny and Angela.

"And some people don't get asked into sixth grade," he remarked casually, "because they can't cut it! Not naming any names, of course!"

Lauren and Kate started laughing. Jenny's face turned red. She slammed her milk carton down on her tray and drops of milk flew all over her and Angela.

"You're a J-E-R-K, Henry Larkin," Jenny said as she stood up. "Everyone knows why *you* don't want Patti to leave Mrs. Mead's class."

Henry stayed calm. He even tipped back on the back legs of his chair and folded his arms across his chest. "Why is that?" he asked.

I could see Patti watching him anxiously.

Jenny looked at Patti with a wicked smile. "Because you two are in *luuuuv*!" Jenny drawled, then waited to see what he would do.

But Henry didn't seem bothered at all.

I think Patti was holding her breath.

"So what?" Henry said to Jenny. "Maybe you're just jealous."

Jenny stopped smiling and stared at him. Patti smiled happily. Lauren and Kate were laughing even harder. I couldn't help it — I started laughing, too. I tried to stop myself, but one giggle escaped, then another and another.

"Oooh! You're all nitwits!" Jenny cried. Then she got up, motioned to Angela, and stomped away with Angela trailing behind.

"Oooh! You're all nitwits!" Kate mimicked Jenny's final words. "*Nitwits!* Give me a break!"

It felt good to laugh with my friends again — even if it wasn't very nice to make fun of Jenny. But *she* had started it, and she had it coming. I was so busy laughing that I almost missed the exchange going on between Patti and Henry.

"Thanks for sticking up for me," Patti said shyly.

"Anytime," Henry said, looking into her eyes. "Really. Anytime at all."

"Patti Larkin," I whispered when she turned back to the group. "Doesn't sound bad at all."

"Don't be ridiculous!" Patti blushed furiously.

"He's still looking at you," I told her.

"Oh, please!" she said softly, without looking back at Henry.

Then the lunch bell rang. As we were gathering

our stuff, Kate reminded us about the Pizza Palace.

"Weren't we going to talk about a way to get John to recycle?" she asked. "Jenny kind of took up all our lunch hour."

"Why don't we meet at Charlie's after school and finish talking about it? Stephanie has some good ideas she can tell us about," Patti said.

"Uh, I can't come this afternoon," I told them. "I promised I'd take all the books and pledges to the library."

"We practically never see you anymore," Lauren complained.

"It's for a good cause," I said, attempting to be cheerful. My reasoning sounded weak, even to me. It was true. This was at least the third time I'd had to cancel plans. As I walked away, I couldn't help wondering what the point was of being a good friend when I hardly had time to spend with my friends!

Chapter
10

At the corner of Hillcrest and Pine the next morning, Patti filled us in on what her parents had said.

"They haven't come to any decisions yet, but they're looking at the books I brought home," she told us as we started riding. "At least there's one good thing about spending my afternoons in sixth grade," she added. "For part of the day, at least, I'm not the tallest girl in the class."

"I told you that you'd like that part," I said, nodding my head.

"But I still feel a lot younger than the other kids, and I'm still not looking forward to all the makeup work I might have to do."

We had auditions for a play the fifth grade was putting on in the morning, so lunchtime rolled around quickly.

"Does anything look good?" Hope said, coming up behind us in line.

"Didn't you bring your own lunch today?" I asked.

"No, I was running late this morning," Hope explained.

"That salad looks good," Patti said, pointing to a pile of greenery in a covered, plastic container.

"Yeah, and they have toasted-cheese sandwiches," Kate told us from farther up in the line.

"I guess I won't starve, then," Hope said, choosing items for her tray.

I paid for my food and carried my tray to our table, wiping some crumbs off the seat before I sat down.

"So, Patti," Hope began, "I've been meaning to ask you how your visits to the sixth-grade class have been going."

"I'd rather talk about the Pizza Palace problem," Patti said.

"That bad, huh?" Hope nodded sympathetically.

"Worse," Patti told her.

Since Patti wanted to change the subject, I jumped right in. "How about picketing the front of the Palace with signs that say, 'Don't eat here. The Pizza Palace doesn't care about the environment!' "

"Or passing out leaflets on recycling in front of

the restaurant," Kate said. "You could do the lettering."

"Let's be careful. I don't think we should make John mad," Hope said. "After all, we still like to eat there."

"Yep," Patti said. "No one makes a pepperoni pizza as good as John does. Ooops, sorry, Hope."

"That's okay. He makes great pineapple-and-bell pepper pizza, too."

"We need to find some *gentle* way to persuade him," Lauren said.

"He said he didn't have time," Kate reminded us.

"*We'll* do it!" I cried. The words were out before I could stop myself. Volunteering was becoming a way of life for me.

"That's true," Hope said. "If we volunteer to help him, there won't be any way he can say no."

"I have another idea," Patti said. "When things are written down on paper, they mean more than if we just say them. What if we make up a petition and gather signatures asking John to start recycling paper, cans, and plastic from the Pizza Palace? *Then* we could offer to help him do it."

"Let's start today after school," I said, my enthusiasm growing. I liked the idea of us all doing a project together.

"We can't," Hope said. "They're expecting us

at the recycling center. Our days are Tuesdays and Thursdays, remember?"

"Sorry, I forgot. I've been kind of busy lately."

"Yeah, it looks like 'volunteer' has replaced 'shopping' as Stephanie's favorite word," Kate teased. "I don't know how she does it."

Even though I had been too busy to see her lately, I could tell Kate was sort of proud of me, anyway. I could hear it in the tone of her voice. The trouble was, I needed a secretary to help me remember my schedule! I groaned and picked up my books.

That afternoon was really tiring at the recycling center. I wasn't sure what was happening to me, but volunteering there this time wasn't nearly as fulfilling as it had been before. The work was all the same — boring. Hope and I had to stack tons of cardboard for the baler. All I wanted was a shower and a good night's sleep.

"I wonder how much effect we're really making against the world recycling problem," I said to Hope as the forklift driver brought over another load of boxes to break down. "I mean, two fifth-graders against a mountain of the world's garbage. It seems hopeless."

"I wonder the same thing myself sometimes," Hope said. "But then I think about all the other volunteers out there. If each person does just a little bit, their efforts add up."

"I guess. I hope someday I get to see what all the efforts add up to," I said. "Right now, all I can think about is taking a shower."

But when I arrived home, Mom was going crazy because she still hadn't done the shopping, and the twins were both screaming at once, and dinner wasn't ready. So instead of a shower, I washed my hands and opened up cans of chili con carne for dinner. Stephanie to the rescue.

And, instead of a nap after dinner, I went with Mom to the grocery store and pushed Emma and Jeremy in the double stroller so that she could do the shopping in peace.

Dad still wasn't home when we got back at nine o'clock — he's a lawyer and sometimes has to work late on a case — so I helped Mom put the groceries away.

"There's a stack of books to be donated to the library in the front hall, Steph," she said. "One of the neighbors dropped them off this afternoon. I'd like to see them gone by tomorrow."

"Sure, Mom. I'll do it after school."

"Thanks for helping me out with the groceries tonight. How about a clothes shopping trip after school on Thursday?" Mom asked. "Dad is going to be home early that day. He said he'd take the twins so that we could do our mother-daughter thing."

"Sounds wonderful," I said, my eyes drooping.

"If you don't mind, I think I'm going to bed." Sure didn't sound like me, did it? I used to love going shopping more than anything. Now, nothing seemed to matter except sleep.

"What about your homework? Oh, no! Did I keep you from doing homework?" Mom asked, a worried expression on her face.

"No, it's okay, Mom," I lied sleepily. "I'll do it in the morning."

"Good night, darling," she said, kissing me. "You were a lifesaver tonight."

"G'night, Mom." I had a warm feeling inside.

I'm not sure if I hit the bed before I went to sleep or if I went to sleep before I hit the bed. I *do* know that I didn't wake up in time to do my homework before school. I also didn't finish even a quarter of it during the announcements that morning.

I was still frantically writing when Mrs. Mead called on me. "Stephanie, would you please put math problem number three on the board?"

I looked at my math book and the words of the problem seemed to swim in front of my eyes. I read, *Mrs. DeVrees has been driving six hours and has gone 431 kilometers. How far do you think she will have driven altogether in ten hours? How far did she drive in the first four hours? What is her average speed in kilometers per hour?*

I hadn't done the problem. I looked at the map

diagram with lines drawn for her route. I didn't know where to start. It didn't even make sense. Even without the pressure of having to do it in class, a word problem like this one sometimes seems to take hours.

I stood up to go to the board, but then I sat down again. "I'm sorry, Mrs. Mead. I didn't understand the problem."

"That's all right, Stephanie. Just put what you do have on the chalkboard, and the class will help you with the rest."

I've never heard such silence in my life. Not one person spoke in the classroom. I imagined that everyone could hear my heart beating, and see the drops of sweat running down the sides of my face.

I know I was blushing. "I didn't do it at all," I finally said, and let out my breath in one puff of air.

"Did you do any of the other problems?"

"No," I whispered, head down.

"That's not like you, Stephanie," Mrs. Mead said.

"I know. I'll do better tomorrow, I promise."

I could feel Lauren's, Kate's, and Patti's eyes practically boring holes in my back. I was mortified, and I knew my friends were really surprised.

I could have told Mrs. Mead that my mother forced me to go to the store with her to take care of the twins, but I knew that wasn't the real excuse. There just wasn't any time left in my niceness schedule for homework. There also wasn't any time for my friends, or for myself.

There was an uncomfortable silence at lunch. I didn't talk much because I was catching up on my homework. I think the others didn't talk much because they didn't know what to say to me. I kept my eyes on my science book. I didn't want to be embarrassed again during class in the afternoon.

Jenny Carlin walked by. I didn't really notice her until she stopped beside me and peered over my shoulder at my book. "Still playing catch-up?" she asked in a sickeningly sweet voice. "I know the perfect person to tutor you on your science homework. Karla Stamos. Would you like me to call her over?"

I ignored her and continued writing down the answers for the review questions at the end of the chapter.

"Be quiet, Jenny," Patti said. "Can't you see Stephanie is working?"

"I can see she totally blew it in class today. I wouldn't want to be her friend right now. Aren't you afraid some of her dumbness might rub off on you?"

"That's enough, Jenny," I said, through clenched teeth. "Everyone is entitiled to a mistake every now and then." I glanced up at her. "Even you."

Jenny took a step back. Her eyes darted from

99

one side to the other. She was probably working up to having "the last word." But when she couldn't think of anything, she stomped away, followed by a silent Angela.

I went back to my homework. The silence around our table resumed.

After school, all I wanted to do was go home and crash, but I knew I had promised to go to the mall. "I guess we'd better go to the mall and start collecting signatures," I said, forcing a false perkiness into my voice.

"We don't have to, Steph," Patti said. "Not if you have to do homework."

"I'll be fine. Don't worry about me," I said brightly. "Let's go!"

"Aren't you even upset about your school-work?" Lauren asked. "I saw your grade on the science test when Mrs. Mead passed them back today. You got a D."

"I'll do better next time," I said.

"You're acting like it doesn't even matter," Kate said, amazed. "One low grade can mess up your whole report card."

I didn't want to talk about it right then. If I did, I thought I might start crying.

Patti walked up to me and put her arm around my shoulder. "Stephanie, is there something that you

want to tell us? You've been kind of . . . different
. . . lately.''

"I sort of miss the old Stephanie," Lauren added.
"Before you went on this goodness kick."

That made me mad. "I'm fine. Leave me alone!"
I said, frowning.

What was wrong with them anyway? Didn't they
realize how lucky they were to have such a nice
person as a friend? I was trying so hard, and they
were telling me I still wasn't good enough!

"Let's go!" I said again.

Of course, people at the mall were happy to sign
the petitions. It didn't take long before we had pages
of signatures. So why wasn't I happier?

Things got even worse the next day. Mrs. Mead
took me aside during recess and gave me one of her
"talks."

"Stephanie, I've noticed that you've been rather
distracted lately," she began. "Would you like to
talk to me about it?"

My mouth felt like it was stuffed with cotton. I
didn't know where to start so I just kept quiet. I shook
my head.

"Getting poor grades on tests and missing homework assignments is very serious," Mrs. Mead went
on. "When a usually good student starts falling behind, I wonder about two things."

"What two things?" I asked, hoping she hadn't guessed about my niceness plan.

She put her arm around my shoulder and guided me to a seat. Then she looked at me for a long moment before she spoke. "I wonder if something is going wrong at home — family problems, or a change in schedule or responsibility." She didn't know how close she was when she mentioned the schedule and change in responsibility idea.

"Or?" I prompted, hoping to get her off of the subject.

She smiled. "Or I wonder if the way I'm teaching a particular subject is just not getting through to the student. Sometimes extra tutoring can help in a case like that."

"Oh, no, Mrs. Mead," I cried, totally embarrassed that she would think I needed tutoring. "I've just been very busy lately. I understand what you're teaching. It's just a time thing. Please don't make me have a tutor. I'll do better. I promise."

"Are you sure you don't want to tell me what brought on this sudden lack of time?" Mrs. Mead asked. "Perhaps you're doing too much fund-raising for the library?"

"Maybe," I said. She didn't even know about the recycling center, the Sea Mammal League, and the Pizza Palace recycling campaign! "Don't worry," I assured her, "I'll be all caught up by tomorrow."

"Fine. I can count on you, then," Mrs. Mead said. "To help you out a little today, though, I'm going to send you to study hall for an hour. You know the rules. If you forget an assignment, you must make it up in study hall."

"That's okay, Mrs. Mead," I said, trying to dredge up something from my niceness plan. "The rules are there to help us."

"It's nice that you're so understanding," she said with a smile.

Understanding, hah! All I wanted to do was escape before the rest of the class came back in and found me talking to the teacher.

I think I did a good job hiding my worries in front of Mrs. Mead and my Sleepover Friends, but I couldn't hide from myself. I was really worried about my homework. I was really worried about my life. My niceness plan was making things worse instead of better.

And even if I'd wanted to talk to one of my friends after school, they were too busy discussing the Pizza Palace.

"I can't wait to see the look on John's face when we show him the petition and offer to help out," Kate was saying as we walked out to the bike racks.

"He's going to be surprised, all right," Lauren said.

"And impressed," Hope said.

Patti didn't join in their conversation. Instead, she was looking at my glum face with concern. She slowed her pace as I dropped farther and farther behind the group.

I was thinking hard. I had to do something about my homework. I had to do something right away. Otherwise, Mrs. Mead was going to assign me a tutor — probably boring Karla Stamos — and I was going to be the laughingstock of 5B.

"Are you okay?" Patti said. "You seem so sad. Can I help?"

"Thanks, Patti," I said, forcing myself to smile. "But this is something I have to take care of on my own."

On my own.

Suddenly I had a great idea — a way to catch up on my homework and keep my promise to Mrs. Mead.

"Are you sure?" Patti continued. "You know you can tell me anything."

"You're the best!" I said, more enthusiastic than I had been all day. "But don't worry. I have it all under control!"

I ran ahead of the others and jumped on my bike. "See you tomorrow," I said and rode off on my bike before they could ask any questions. I didn't tell them where I was going. I just left.

"Hey, Steph," I heard Hope call, "I'll ride with you!" But I didn't stop. I knew what I was going to do. I was going to go to the library and catch up on my schoolwork without the twins screaming in the background.

I was also going to unload five pounds of leaflets that I had been carrying around in my backpack for the past week.

That's just what I did. I found the farthest corner in the back of the library, behind the research books, and set up my stuff on the table.

I don't know how long I worked, but after awhile I started seeing the end. Science, social studies, language — the finished papers piled up to my right.

I was really proud of myself for catching up so quickly. See, I told myself, I can do it. I can do it all. I'm like superwoman. All I needed was a little time to myself to get my work done. I can carry a full load at school *and* be a community volunteer, too.

I had everything under control. My schoolwork — I had taken the responsibility for improving my grades myself by coming to the library. My volunteer jobs — I had made a plan to become a nicer, more giving person, and it was working.

If only I could keep my eyes open. . . .

"Stephanie! Stephanie! There you are! Thank goodness!"

The next thing I knew I was being shaken awake. The harsh fluorescent light hurt my eyes. I blinked, then rubbed my neck. It was stiff from lying on my arm. Where was I? Then I remembered.

I must have fallen asleep, but what was all the noise and commotion? My left foot tingled as I tried to shake it, and me, awake.

My mother hugged me tightly — what was she doing here? I looked over her shoulder to see the head librarian, *two police officers*, and a cleaning woman! The clock on the wall said it was almost eight o'clock! I had come to the library at three — five hours earlier!

"Oh, no," I groaned. "I'm sorry, I forgot to call you."

"That isn't even the half of it! Get your things, young lady, and come get in the car," Mom said briskly. "We have a lot of talking to do!"

She thanked the police officers for their help, and apologized to the librarian for all the trouble I'd caused.

Groggily, all the way home in the silent car, I tried to figure out why I was in so much trouble.

As we drove into the driveway I noticed Lauren, Hope, Kate, and Patti all lined up on my front porch. Their bikes were in the grass, and they all had identical worried expressions on their faces.

"Has something happened?" I asked anxiously.

"Was someone in an accident? Is it the twins?"

"No, Mrs. Campbell is watching the twins," Mom told me.

"Oh, no, it's not Bullwinkle, is it, Lauren? Did something happen to your dog?"

"It's *you*, dummy!" Lauren said. "*You're* the one we're worried about! Where have you been all afternoon?"

I looked around, the situation finally dawning on me. "Well, I, uh, was in the library doing my homework."

"When you left school I thought you were going to the recycling center," Hope said.

"Oh, no," I said, slapping my forehead. "I was supposed to go to the recycling center today." The nightmare was getting worse.

"Hope called me to find out where you were," Mom said. "I didn't know because you had told me you were coming home to go shopping with me."

I groaned and put my head on my arms. "I know I'm supposed to call," I mumbled at the table. "I was so involved with my homework that I forgot."

"You've been forgetting a lot of things lately," Mom continued. "Like how to take care of yourself. We've been going crazy this afternoon looking for you."

"After Hope called, then what happened?" I had to ask.

"Well, I called Lauren, Kate, and Patti to find out if they knew where you were," Mom said. "Of course they didn't — so we called the police, and searched the mall, the park, the school grounds — all of the places where you hang out."

I wanted to die.

"We also checked the Sea Mammal League," Hope said.

"We were really scared," Lauren told me.

"We thought you were kidnapped, or worse," Kate said.

"We thought we'd never see you again," whispered Patti, tears in her eyes. Tears came to my eyes, too.

"The library was a last resort," Mom said. "By that time, we were all hysterical."

"Did you find her?" Dad asked, bursting into the room.

"She's here," Mom told him. "Your father has been driving up and down every street in Riverhurst looking for your bike," she told me hoarsely.

"I'm sorry, Mom, Dad, everybody," I said, starting to cry.

"I'm just glad nothing happened to my baby," Mom said, hugging me again. Soon she was crying, Dad was crying, and everyone else in the room — including Mrs. Campbell — was getting misty-eyed.

"I didn't do it on purpose," I sobbed. "I never

meant to scare you. I just had to find a quiet place to catch up on my homework. I've been kind of busy lately."

"Too busy," Dad said, standing up and wiping his eyes. "There are going to be some new rules around here, starting tonight."

"Am I grounded?" I asked. I was almost hoping I was, so that I could get out of some of my commitments gracefully.

"No, you're not grounded," Dad said. "But there will be no more outside volunteer work for charities during the school year."

"And no more extra chores around the house," Mom added.

"And you will call first before you go anywhere after school!" Dad said. "No matter what, even if it's only to stop by Charlie's for ice cream."

Mom took my face in her hands and kissed me on the nose. "Your only activity from now on will be homework. Got it?"

"Okay," I said, almost starting to cry again in relief. "I promise."

Then I started to get a little worried. "But what about the sleepovers?" I said hesitantly.

"I don't know," Mom said, looking at Dad.

I looked at Patti, Lauren, and Kate. Our eyes grew wide and round with horror.

"I think we should cancel the one tomorrow

night and then see how it goes next week. If things are back to normal, then we'll see," Dad said.

"NO!" we all shouted at once.

"Oh, please, Mom, Dad," I begged. "I promise I'll get back on track. I'll have all weekend to get rested up! I've finished all of my homework!"

"We won't stay up late. We promise," Lauren said.

Kate added her own promise. "We'll make sure Stephanie doesn't eat too much junk food or get too excited."

"Or play any wild games," said Patti.

Mom smiled. "That doesn't sound like much of a sleepover."

"I'll do whatever you want," I said. "But please don't cancel the sleepover."

Dad smiled, too.

I knew then that everything was going to be all right.

Chapter
11

"Yesterday was pretty exciting," Lauren said at morning recess the next day.

Lauren, Kate, Patti, Hope, and I stood near the big oak tree in the middle of the playground.

"I'm glad you're okay, Stephanie," Hope said. "What happened yesterday made me think about my own schedule. I'm going to cut down my hours at the recycling center, too. It's fun, but it does take a lot of time away from other things I want to do. I barely have time to spend with my friends — you guys."

"I know what you mean. I guess I've really been doing too much lately," I admitted.

"But some of it was really good," Kate said. "Like our petition for the Pizza Palace."

"Right," Lauren said. "We counted the number of people who signed and we have two hundred names! All those signatures look very impressive."

"That should be enough to show John that we're serious," I said.

"Enough?" Lauren exclaimed. "We should do this to every business in Riverhurst!"

I felt her forehead the same way Kate had felt mine when I started going overboard last week. "Is this the same Lauren who went to the recycling center only because she didn't have anything better to do?" I teased.

"Well, I changed my mind a little," Lauren said. "Recycling is important, and I can't believe how much recyclable material the businesses of Riverhurst waste every day."

Patti twirled a piece of grass around her finger. "I think if we can just get John to agree, we will have done our part. Maybe later, during the summer, we could add another business to our list."

"You're right. If the petition persuades John to agree, we will have done enough." I think my comment surprised me more than anyone!

Suddenly I had another of my great ideas. An idea that might help persuade Patti's parents not to skip her into sixth grade. I waited until Patti had to go to the science room to discuss a Quarks project, then I gathered everyone else together to tell them my plan.

They all thought it was a terrific idea, too!

Without Patti knowing what we were doing, we quietly worked on my plan throughout the afternoon. By the end of school on Friday, we were all pleased with the results of our efforts and were ready for the sleepover that night.

There was just one thing left that I had to talk my newly strict parents into letting me do before the sleepover at Patti's house. Luckily my folks said they could probably stand one more Friday-night pizza dinner at the Palace, so we met Lauren, Kate, Hope, and Patti there.

While we were there we presented our signed petition to John.

"So you see, John," Lauren began, "your customers are very concerned about the environment. We think they would back you one hundred percent if you started a program. Business might even increase."

"I thought I told you girls that recycling was too much work and not cost-effective," John grumbled.

"Saving the environment isn't always cheap," Hope said. "But it's worth it."

"I don't even know what to do to get started," John said. "You girls started something, and now you expect *me* to finish it."

"Don't get mad, John," I said. "We'll help you get started. If you agree, we'll start tonight."

He looked at his assistant, who shrugged his

shoulders and smiled at us. Then he looked out into the restaurant and was surprised to see most of the customers watching him, waiting for his decision.

"Oh, all right!" he said. "I'll do it, but I'm going to need help. Anyone who wants to come in and work for a couple of hours, I'll give you a free pizza with the works."

A cheer went up from the customers. My friends and I couldn't help jumping for joy.

"We'll be your first volunteers!" I offered.

And that's just what we did. Even Dad rolled up his shirtsleeves and dug into the trash with us.

Dealing with pizza garbage is pretty icky — okay, *major* icky — but we soon had everything stored and bagged neatly. Then we had a huge pizza to celebrate. We got everything on it except meatballs and pepperoni, so Hope could eat it, too.

I knew I shouldn't get any more involved, but I couldn't stop myself. When we were almost finished eating, I turned to my parents. "Dad, Mom, would it be all right if I volunteered to come once a week and help John out?" I asked. "I feel responsible for getting his recycling program started, and I should help out."

"You may do it if it doesn't interfere with your schoolwork," Dad said. Mom nodded her head.

I didn't expect anyone else to sign up, because I knew they were fed up with me coaxing them into anything. So I was really surprised when Lauren tossed her napkin onto her plate and said, "I think I'll come, too. How about you guys?" she asked the others. "What if we agreed to do it for only one month? That should be enough to get John started."

"Okay," Kate agreed. "Besides, someone has to keep an eye on Stephanie."

They all laughed, and I smiled, too.

We finished our pizza and Mom and Dad dropped us off at Patti's house. Once there, we grabbed our snacks for later in the evening and trooped all the way upstairs to the Jenkins' attic. It's a great place for a sleepover. Patti had already moved her parents' small TV up there.

"I'm glad you're spending the night with us tonight, Hope," I said.

"Yeah," Kate agreed.

"Me, too," Lauren said.

"Me, three," Patti said.

Hope looked around at us with a shy smile on her face. "Thanks," she said. "I like being here."

"Well, hey, we ought to do something to celebrate," Kate suggested. "Let's all scare ourselves silly by watching 'Friday Night Chillers' on Channel 21."

"Aw, do we have to?" Lauren said, grabbing her sleeping bag and pulling it around her.

"Oh, why not?" Patti said. "We can always ignore the scary parts and talk instead."

We all laid out our sleeping bags, jockeying for position on the old rugs on the attic floor. Then we turned on the TV and settled down for some serious shivers.

An hour later we were all laughing as Kate turned the TV off. "Those giant man-eating ants were the dumbest things I ever saw," Lauren howled. "I've seen scarier insects in our garden!"

"Ahhh! Ahhh! They're coming to get me!" I yelled, rolling on my back and kicking my feet in the air like the heroine did in the movie.

"May I have everyone's attention?" Kate asked a few minutes later when we had calmed down. "Stephanie," she said, "I just want to say that although it has been really *nice* of you to do all of this volunteering, we can't help missing the old Stephanie — the one who put her friends first."

My mouth formed an "O" of surprise, and my eyes started to well up with tears as Lauren continued. "We're asking you to sign us up as a charity, so you can devote at least some of your time to us!"

I smiled and giggled sheepishly.

"Yeah," Patti said. "Anyway, we just wanted you to know that we like you the way you are — were. You don't have to prove to *us* that you're a good person."

Kate pulled the copy of *Teen Topics* with the

quiz out from behind her back. "We found the quiz and all the notes you wrote about your plan to become a nice person. We think you're already one of the nicest people around. Don't we, gang?"

Everyone cheered, including me, as Kate tore out the article from the magazine and ripped it up into tiny pieces. But did they really mean it? Was I really okay the way I was? I was really getting tired of being nice to dumb old Jenny Carlin!

I stood up and took a little bow. "All right, now *I* have an announcement to make," I said. "I am no longer going to try to be nice all the time."

More cheers. Lauren put her fingers in her mouth and whistled loudly.

"I'm actually relieved to be quitting the library, the recycling center, and the Sea Mammal League. And I want you guys to know that you don't have to come help me at the Pizza Palace if you don't want to. I know you offered to just to be nice."

"That's not true, Steph," Lauren said. "Believe it or not, some of your community spirit has rubbed off on all of us. We'll be there with you every Saturday morning for a whole month."

"Besides," Kate added, "what a great way to get a free pizza!"

"Speaking of food," Lauren said. "Is anybody hungry?"

An instant later, four pillows hit Lauren in the

head. But she still beat us downstairs to the kitchen.

A few minutes later, we were all sitting around the kitchen table sipping shakes that Hope had whipped up for us in the blender. They were made out of raspberry sherbet and crushed fresh fruit.

"We have a surprise for you, Patti," I announced.

"A way to get me out of sixth grade?" she asked eagerly.

"Well, it might be a way of persuading your parents not to skip you — just like we persuaded John to start recycling," I said. Then I took out the petition we had gotten signed by almost every kid in the fifth-grade class.

"It's asking your parents to let you stay in 5B," Lauren told her.

Patti was overwhelmed. She just sat there staring at all the signatures. "Look," she said. "Even Jenny Carlin and Ginger Kinkaid signed."

I grinned. "We had to do a little arm-twisting on Jenny. But I think she figured if she couldn't skip, then she didn't want anyone else to, either."

"The reason doesn't matter," Hope said. "The signature does."

"And Henry signed *four times*," Patti sighed happily. "This will do it! I'll show it to my parents in the morning. I'm positive this will convince them to let me stay where I am!"

The next morning, after we'd eaten breakfast, we all sat on the front porch to wait for Patti's parents to get ready to take us home. The Jenkinses were going to a museum that day, so they were dropping us off on the way.

The minute they walked out the door, Patti showed them the petition.

"Goodness, you've gone to a lot of trouble," Mrs. Jenkins said.

"Actually, Lauren, Stephanie, Kate, and Hope went to all the trouble. I didn't know anything about the petition," Patti explained. "All I *do* know is that I don't feel right in sixth grade. The teacher is fine and the kids are getting better, I guess. But it's not *fun*, the way every class has been up until now. Getting an education should be *fun*, right?"

"There are a lot of aspects to an education," Mrs. Jenkins said. "And I suppose having fun is one of them."

Patti paced around in front of her parents. She had that little frown on her face that she had worn most of the time lately.

I knew it wasn't the time to break into their conversation or add any advice of our own. This was something that had to be worked out by Patti and her parents. We had done everything we could. Now we had to wait.

Finally Patti stopped pacing and looked at her

parents. "I *could* do it," she said. "I could skip into sixth grade and I'm sure I could catch up and do well. I'm sure I could make a few friends there eventually and I'm sure I'd survive."

"Survival isn't exactly what we had in mind," Mr. Jenkins said. "We want school to be a good experience for you. After all, if you're enjoying yourself, your grades will be much better naturally. We don't want to force you into doing something that you don't want to do."

Patti looked from one to the other. We all held our breaths.

"Does this mean . . . ?" she started to say.

"It means that we have come to a decision," Mrs. Jenkins told her.

"This has been a difficult decision for us," Mr. Jenkins said. "We want you to have a good education, but we also want you to be happy."

"I would be happier in 5B with my friends," Patti said quietly.

"And it seems," Mr. Jenkins said, holding out the petition, "that your friends would be happier with you there, too."

"The decision, Patti," Mrs. Jenkins added, "is that we should let you make your own decision on this one. If you're mature enough to skip a grade, you're mature enough to decide if you want to or not."

Mr. Jenkins nodded his head. Then they waited for Patti to speak. She could hardly believe it. All these weeks of worry, and now the decision was left entirely up to her. Finally she looked around at all of us and back at her parents. "Mom, Dad, I love you," she said. "I choose 5B!"

"Yay!" Kate shouted. "First we get the old Stephanie back, and now Patti is staying with us!"

"This is the best thing that could ever happen!" I shouted.

"We're all together again!" Lauren said, jumping up and down.

"I know you did the right thing, Patti," Hope said. "I don't know if I could have been brave enough to decide something that important on my own."

Patti smiled, then winked. "Oh, it was easy," she said. "I had a little help from my friends." She reached over and took Kate's hand. Kate reached for Hope. Hope reached for me. I grabbed Lauren, and she took Patti's other hand to complete the circle. "Ready? One . . . two . . . three!" Patti said.

Then we all shouted at once: "Sleepover Friends forever!"

#36 Presenting Patti

I felt Stephanie shaking my arm. "Go on, Patti," she whispered. "Didn't you hear her call your name?"

Everyone in the auditorium was clapping. I took a deep breath, stood up, and walked toward the steps. It seemed as if it took me about an hour to get up on stage.

I smoothed out my speech and faced the audience. I looked at the front row, just as Lauren had told me to do. Kate gave me the "okay" sign with her thumb and forefinger. Lauren was making a goofy face. Stephanie just winked at me. I couldn't even look at Henry.

It's now or never, I told myself. *Just go slow, and take it easy.* My mouth was so dry, I could hardly talk.

"Hi," I said. "My name is Patti Jenkins, and this is my, uh, my — " Then everything went black!

SLEEPOVER FRIENDS™

by Susan Saunders

Available wherever you buy books...or use this order form.

THE BABY-SITTERS CLUB®

Collect Them All!

by Ann M. Martin

The seven girls at Stoneybrook Middle School get into all kinds of adventures...with school, boys, and, of course, baby-sitting!

For a complete listing of all the Baby-sitter Club titles write to:
Customer Service at the address below.

Available wherever you buy books...or use this order form.